LOVING THE ROGUE

AMANDA KIMBERLEY

For my pack that gives me much pride.

ABOUT LOVING THE ROGUE

Nothing's fair in love and war.
AND...
The only way to save her was to make her his
Treasure.

Takoda, Alpha of The Shoshone Tribe, knew the laws were clear when you came upon a lone pup during the rebellion. You either take the babe in as one of your own or banish them to a part of the country where they could do no harm.

She couldn't have been more than 14 or 15, young enough to train in The Shoshone ways, but old enough to give the young Omegas in his pack reason to hate her. And because of that reason alone, he couldn't take this girl called Treasure into his fold. So he did the next best thing. He entrusted her upbringing to his friend, Nayati, Alpha of the Cheyenne tribe.

All was supposed to fall into place until the Cheyenne tribe had a falling out with his Shoshone one. He'd have to fight against the one person he wanted to save unless he made her his Treasure.

PROLOGUE

It was the bloodiest battle he'd seen as a born shifter in all of his existence. They lost more pride members during this now deemed Civil Were War than they had in any other war, including the Were Rebellion in the 14th century. As usual, the war that every shifter was now involved with was started by the wolves. Hence, the bastards got to name the war. And that never rested well with the pride nations, nor Takoda.

Sure, he'd been in squabbles among the shifter packs in the Americas before. And some of them were damned close to being called an all-out war. But they were nothing compared to this. Nothing where thousands of shifters died at the hands of other shifters.

As he peered out into the dense forest, he

couldn't hear any signs of life. Not even a cricket was singing.

"So much death." He found himself saying this aloud to the gods while he shook his head. Nayati nodded in agreement as the two of them continued their trek through the thickly dense forest.

Takoda and Nayati were appointed by the council to comb the territory for survivors now that the war was coming to an end. Sadly, most of their hunts led to more of a recovery mission as they witnessed countless lifeless bodies in the mountains of Wyoming. It seemed almost everyone left chose to join one of their prides. Aside from Ocean's tribal wolf pack and Donovan's family, there were two small cougar prides living in their general area of Wyoming in this current day. Takoda's Shoshone Pack grew by the numbers daily. Because he was the strongest and oldest Alpha in Wyoming, the shifters that found themselves prideless joined him or Nayati's pride. He was the Alpha of the Cheyenne Pack and was the second largest in all the inter-mountain region.

"Do you think we got them all, Takoda?" Nayati asked him as he turned over some brush that was placed strangely around a cave entrance.

"We can't be too sure. Lenox's New England pack grew in strong numbers once he took over Moytoy's pack while he was here. I still don't know how he was able to reverse his son Gavin's spell so quickly. It's hard to believe that a werewitch could find such a spell to be able to shift again. I'm surprised at most of Moytoy's pack, though. I was certain they'd remain loyal to Honaw rather than follow Lenox here."

"Well, I guess most of them still side with him even though no laws were broken. I hear that Lenox managed to survive this war, even though most of his original pack did not. That werewolf's got as many lives as us cats."

Takoda removed some more of the brush from the cave entrance and went in. To his surprise, he encountered a girl. She couldn't have been more than 19 kitten years, as his best guess. Her long hair spread around her shoulders and shielded most of her face from him as she coward from the sight of him entering the cave. Her almond-shaped eyes widened as he stepped closer to her.

"Please! Don't hurt me! I'll do anything you say. I swear. My Alpha is dead, and I may be young, but I know the laws." She scurried away from him, towards a corner in the cave.

Her cognac-colored eyes darted in every direction as she spoke. Clearly, she was looking for a quick escape from Takoda. But when Nayati entered the cave, the girl curled back up into a ball and proceeded to sway back and forth in the tiny dark corner she retreated to in the cave. Her eyes and face appeared to be in a fixated, catatonic state. She must have realized she had no way to escape and fell into a panic. Takoda felt a tremendous weight forming deep within his chest for the poor girl. Because of everything he'd seen in this war, sympathy was a fleeting feeling for both him and Nayati. Too many times, he'd come across a field, praying to the gods that at least one of them from the massive amount of bodies could be saved. There were either no survivors or a shifter who refused to be saved most of the time.

The pain grew heavier and deepened as he inched closer. It was becoming harder for him to breathe.

"I'll be your slave if I have to. That won't bother me. I just don't want a sentence of banishment. Please!" Her eyes fixated on the cave wall in front of her.

Once Takoda was close enough, he kneeled down beside the teen and brushed her wavy and unruly hair away from her eyes. She shuttered at the gesture.

"It's okay, nüttüühai ~ nittüühai." He started.

Her eyes suddenly locked onto his. Something he assumed wouldn't happen so easily. He then noticed she searched for the meaning behind his words.

Crap! She doesn't speak our language! I was so sure she did!

"I'm sorry. I said, dear. It was silly of me to

assume you spoke Shoshone, and I have no intention of hurting you. What's your name?"

"Treasure."

"That's a pretty name. I'm Takoda, Alpha of the Shoshone pride here in Wyoming."

"I know of you." She said as she swallowed hard and concentrated her gaze back towards the wall. "You are a mighty Alpha warrior, and I'd be honored to be taken into your pride and work for you as you see fit."

Treasure.

It was a beautiful name for a beautiful girl. Takoda was in awe of this girl's essence that seemed to drip from within every word she spoke. Though calculated and unsure of trust, her speech also seemed to radiate throughout the cave, giving him a sense of warmth in the dank surroundings.

All his thoughts were about protecting her from any more harm that would come to her in this god-forsaken war. He hated to see someone so young having to make such hard decisions. And though he felt lucky to have stumbled onto her, so he was able to protect her, sadly, that meant he needed to protect her from his own pride of Omegas.

Takoda hadn't chosen a Luna Queen yet. He didn't want to mate with any of the Omegas in his pack. But that didn't mean they all weren't trying to vie for the position, kicking and swiping at each other to win his affection. To have another female in the mix, especially one so young, could make things hard for Treasure.

All the Omegas beat on each other. It was an unfortunate standard in prides to show dormancy over the other Omegas. And Takoda couldn't bear to see this Treasure go through any of that. The mere thought of her hurt made him want to pummel the rocks in front of him.

His only choice would be to ask another Alpha to take her in. Nayati already had a Luna Queen, making him the most logical choice to take in a young Omega. Treasure would be safe in his pride.

"Take me with you? Please? I can't survive on my own. I'm not strong enough." The girl said as she latched onto his arm and let out a breath.

A sense of warmth washed over him, and Takoda smiled at the girl. Of all the split decisions he had to make about rogues in this war, this one seemed to be the easiest of all. Her touch was gentle, soft. She wouldn't hurt any of their prides. If anything, she'd be a great asset as he and Nayati trained her for adulthood.

"Hang tight, dear. We will fix this. I need to talk to Nayati over here first." He said to her in a faint whisper while patting the back of her hand that latched onto his arm.

She released her grip as Takoda turned to face his lifelong friend. The warmth that he felt from her seemed to dissipate all too quickly, making Takoda mourn for the moment's loss with her.

"I already see where this is going. I get what you are thinking, but is that really a good idea?" He said with outstretched palms.

"Nayati, you, more than anyone I know, have come to understand how my Omegas act. They'd try to kill her the first chance they got. The only way to protect her is to place her in a pride that already has an established Luna Queen."

Nayati let out a long breath and crossed his arms.

"You do realize we wouldn't be having this conversation if you took on a mate."

"I'm not into any of the Omegas—you get that —right?." Takoda said as he shrugged his shoulders.

"The forever perpetual bachelor," Nayati said as he shook his head and chuckled.

"Alright, fine. I'll take the kid in. But with two conditions. One, I can tell that you have some sort of protectorate bond with her, so you will have to be in her life in some capacity while she is in my pride. And two, once she becomes of age, she should become a part of your pride. This is non-negotiable. Because, in all honesty, I've never seen you want to take on such a protectorate role with a female before. I am certain some time with this girl will help you figure out what you want in a fated mate.

The gods know you haven't been successful looking for just a mate."

Takoda let out a long breath before answering his friend. He was right. Something about the girl was different, and Takoda couldn't figure out why he had such an affinity to want to keep her safe. None of the other casualties meant anything to him before, but this girl did. He was completely compelled to keep her safe from all the blood and gore of this horrible war that would not solve anything among the shifter race. It was in a shifter's innate nature to fight for territory. And his heart sank at the thought of this Treasure being caught in the middle of it all.

"You are right. There is something different about Treasure. But she's only a cub. I couldn't possibly take care of a kitten of her age. I don't know the first thing. That is why I'm asking for your help."

"And I am offering it so long as you take her back into your fold once she becomes a full-fledged adult. The law has always stated that whoever comes upon the lone first—"

"Is the one that must take them in. I know. I remember. I helped write that into law if you remember correctly." Takoda said as he let out a sigh. "Fine, deal." He clasped his best friend's forearm with his hand, and Nayati returned the clasp with his own as a symbol of their solidified agreement.

ONE

About a year and a half had passed since the Civil Were War started. The war, led by the werewolves, extended into all the shifter races and nearly decimated the entire shifter community. War reduced prides and packs that once boasted thousands of members. Now? They dwindled to a mere hundred almost overnight once the fighting began.

Takoda didn't want to see such devastation again in his existence and often prayed to the gods that peace would remain for a lot longer than the six months that'd already come to pass. Living in harmony proved a goal he always wanted to spread in his community after The Were Rebellion. They successfully kept the peace for centuries—that is, until Lenox screwed everything up. The Civil Were

War wasn't something that any of the shifters wanted. Especially since many of them had seen the devastation firsthand in The Were Rebellion. And also because The Common Trifecta law was never broken. Hence, the war was pointless. But here they all were, fighting to stay alive. Some were still bickering, and Takoda lacked the authority and control over many neighboring prides to squelch the feuding.

Shifters lived decades, sometimes centuries longer than normal humans. And like humans, they doted on their family with love and affection. They also showed a great sense of dedication and devotion to the ones they loved. But shifters possessed one huge character flaw. They are prone to squabbles. Takoda had been lucky before the war and managed to stay out of a lot of fighting between territories. Of course, it always helps when your nearest shifter neighbor is your best friend. But recently, even Nayati was falling prey to bickering. This recent misunderstanding he has had with his lifelong friend, Nayati, threw Takoda for a loop. The growing rift between them seemed to come out of nowhere because no matter how much the prides and packs around the two of them argued, Nayati always seemed to have Takoda's back. Until now.

Nayati led an argument that all of Wyoming should be his territory. He thought this partly because his pack had grown in numbers over the past six months, something most prides or packs still struggled with, even with the war coming to an end. But his primary reason for wanting all of Wyoming was because his tribe was indigenous to the land. In contrast, Takoda and the lone wolf known as Donovan settled here sometime after Nayati had.

At first, Takoda assumed the great council would dismiss Nayati's claims. And simply because Takoda's ancestors lived on half of the Wyoming territory so many centuries ago, it became too difficult to distinguish in the Shoshone and Cheyenne tribes, which pride had settled on the land first. The land, especially Mount Sacagawea, remained a shared and neutral living territory for the Shoshone and Cheyenne tribal prides.

Unfortunately, the meeting with the council didn't work out how Takoda had hoped. Nayati convinced many of the elders that Takoda and Donovan should be banished from the state if they had no intention of submitting to Nayati. Some of the council even went further to suggest that if Takoda and Donovan wanted to stay in Wyoming, they should fight the now newly deemed *ultimate Alpha* Nayati for the territory.

Of course, Takoda thought this was crazy, especially since Takoda was the one who'd had numerous recruits when the war started. His pride was the strongest out of all the neighboring states involved in The Civil Were War. Sadly, that meant he'd taken the most gigantic hit in casualties. He had been trying to reason with Nayati and the elders of the council for the last six months. The talks, however, grew less and less peaceful—and this was to no one's surprise. Once Lenox, a powerful Alpha originating from the north, started the war, Nayati changed. No one wanted Lenox in their territory, especially after discovering he killed Rogan in cold blood right before the war began. But both Takoda and Donovan thought it best to allow Lenox to reside in Wyoming with his remaining pack. It was the best way to monitor Lenox to make sure he wasn't breaking any more laws.

However, allowing such a shifter into Wyoming proved to be something both Takoda and Donovan now regretted making. Ever since the bloody battles of the Civil Were War a year ago, Takoda, Donovan, and Ocean took in refugees. Lenox proposed he'd do the same, but he mostly gave the recruits to Nayati.

Lately, Lenox began filling Nayati's head with lies since he'd come to Wyoming. And it seemed all Nayati talked of in the past six months was about being the *ultimate Alpha* of the prides and packs of the Equality State. He became obstinate and spoke in ways that made him seem as if he were drunk on power. This wasn't like Nayati. They'd been friends for decades, and not once did Nayati ever seek to gain territory or power. He was content with the pride the gods provided him. Nayati, the always calm one. He was the one more at peace with the pipe at council meetings and had a gift for being the least strong-headed of the bunch in Wyoming.

Takoda tried to sober Nayati's thoughts. But everything seemed to come to a head when the day came to bring Treasure into Takoda's fold. She was supposed to be in Takoda's pride once she came of age. For their traditions, 21 human years was of age. It was what both he and Nayati shook on almost two years ago.

That day, Takoda began reminiscing about the girl Treasure. The one they both saved and how much Takoda still had an intense urge to keep the girl, now a full-fledged woman, protected. The feud made Takoda contemplate strange things that had never crossed his mind before. He didn't want Treasure in such a toxic situation where Nayati and Takoda grew at odds. If it were up to just Takoda and not the pride, he'd skip the formalities, take her in, and flee Wyoming just to keep her safe.

Perhaps those thoughts had something to do with him still remembering their first meeting when she was 19. Maybe it also had to do with the growing bond they began to share with one another over the past year and a half that Nayati allowed them to bond. Either way, he needed her safe from Nayati and his wrath.

Each time Takoda brought up taking Treasure

into his fold, Nayati seemed to keep making excuses. It had gotten so bad that Takoda only saw Treasure a handful of times in the past six months, and Takoda began to worry that Nayati wouldn't keep his promise. The idea of losing her altogether hallowed out his stomach. And it also made his chest ache with a pain he'd never experienced in all of his shifter years of existence.

The friendship that Takoda had with her bloomed into something a lot different now that she became a full-fledged adult shifter. It was customary that the Alpha leader goes with her on her first hunt as an adult. Both Takoda and Treasure planned date after date for this hunt in the past six months. Still, every time the night was to arrive, Nayati came up with some council meeting that Takoda, as an Alpha, needed to attend. Therefore, both Treasure and Takoda were forced to reschedule the sacred event.

Tonight was supposed to be the night, as far as what was planned between just the two of them. He'd been looking forward to taking Treasure out for her first hunt for months. But now, with this huge rift between him and Nayati, Takoda told Treasure to keep their first hunt a secret from Nayati and the rest of the pride. The plan was that she'd sneak outside Nayati's compound and meet Takoda on the other side of the mountain to hunt.

A strange feeling shot through Takoda's body as

he tried to button his shirt for this momentous occasion. He never raised a litter of his own and figured that what he experienced was just nerves for the night to come. He assumed every father has this experience when letting their children out to face the big, bad world. But the fact was, he didn't raise her. In fact, when he met her, he didn't know the first thing about taking care of a teen, which was why he had Takoda take her to begin with. What was strange to him was the experience coming over him seemed more like what he expected to feel on a first date. Though they'd never done more than hug each other, the feeling coming over him seemed more than anything he had experienced in his short and relatively dull existence as a male.

Sex with the Omegas in his pride wasn't foreign to him because he occasionally needed to scratch that itch. But an itch wasn't anything like what his father once told him about love. During Takoda's first council meeting, when he was a young kitten, his father explained to him about fated mates.

Son, being with your fated mate is as easy as breathing. I'm not saying that everything will come easy between you both. But when you squabble, it will be nothing like the fights over territory. You will both be at peace once you've had time to express your own peace to the only person who understands you completely—and that's your fated mate.

He shook his head and tried to eradicate the

thoughts creeping into his mind. Takoda wasn't going on a date with her. This hunt wasn't a date. She was a rogue cat he was taking in as part of his own pride.

His?

The thought didn't cross him until now. And maybe it was because he never looked at the Omegas as *his.* They were just part of the pride he accepted—part of the pride he inherited from his father.

But Treasure is all mine.

She seemed different to him. A true treasure to his pride. She brought him so much joy and wisdom when they'd talk for long hours about the pride members and the role she'd play in Takoda's compound. They often spoke of the dreams they'd envisioned with the pride once the war ended. He ran his pride far different from Nayati. Treasure was always eager to learn the various nuances between the two prides. They were the closest to a family she had known since her entire pack was killed in the war. He couldn't wait to introduce her to the fold as part of his pride and share her vast knowledge and skills.

Takoda looked in the full-length mirror in front of him and sucked in a breath as he fussed with his hair to get it to look good. It was the first time he ever wanted to impress a girl. He had never done this with the Omegas in his inherited pride. Never.

And now this girl? The one who wasn't even officially in his pack yet because she was still considered part of Nayati's? Was making him entertain ideas he'd never thought possible before.

Am I falling in love with Treasure?

TWO

After four more attempts at passing his fingers through his hair, he finally made his way outside to meet with Treasure.

"Hey, Takoda! I finally broke free. I gave Nayati a bullshit story that I was going out to dinner with my cousin that had just flown in to see me. He agreed to let me go, but he didn't want me to be more than a couple of hours, and I doubt that will be enough time to hunt."

"It is traditionally supposed to take up the whole evening," Takoda said with a slight frown.

"Well, how about we go out for dinner and reschedule again?" Treasure said with a sigh before continuing. "I really don't think he wants to let me go."

"I'm wondering the same thing. But that doesn't mean we can't have a little fun. Come on. This large rock up ahead near the trails is the perfect place to leave our clothes once we shift. Race you!"

He took off as quick as the words came from his lips.

"Hey, no fair! That's cheating!" She said with a thunderous giggle.

He reached the rock in a matter of minutes but tripped on a root protruding from the ground of a nearby tree. He quickly tumbled to the earth. Treasure was on his heels and tripped over the same root, causing her to fall on top of him. A fluttering sensation rose within his belly as her body pressed into his, and he found his arms wrapping themselves around her waist instinctually.

"Serves you right that karma took a bite out of you." Treasure said while giggling once more.

Her lips were a breath from his, so inviting, so tempting. He tried to reason with his cougar, making the animal fully aware that he shouldn't kiss her. It would complicate matters further with Nayati. The problem was that his cougar, body, and mind betrayed him as he cupped her cheek and crashed his lips onto hers without further thought.

She tasted like vanilla, a flavor he now loved and couldn't get enough of. His tongue traced the bottom seam of her lips and gave it a gentle bite. Treasure's muscles tensed to his touch at first. However, as he began to skillfully suck on her bottom lip, her body softened into the kiss. A guttural growl came over him as she made small circles on his chest with her thumbs.

Her hands slinked up to his hair and laced behind his head as her kisses began growing needy, possessive. And his inner cougar purred to attention once she ground her hips into his dick, straining at the zipper of his jeans. She rained kisses along the side of his jawline until her lips met his ear lobe. Goosebumps littered his skin as she gave the lobe a lick before sucking on it. Her palm trailed down the length of his body and cupped his balls. He couldn't feel anything but the growing heat between them and his erection that hardened with each of her strokes.

"Fuck, Treasure," he said before a moan escaped his lips. "You feel so good. I want you."

"I want you too, Takoda." Her voice was silky, like her lips.

She started to fumble with the button and zipper on his jeans. Treasure released his cock from its confined compartment, and she stroked its length as she sucked on the tip. The incredible sensations she was making her tongue perform caused him to gyrate in unison with her movements. She felt so good that he knew he'd come before Takoda ever had the chance to be inside her, and he wasn't having any of that.

He rolled her underneath him and straddled her thighs.

"It's my turn." He said as he ran a finger down her cheek to the button of her shirt just under her gorgeous cleavage. "I want to kiss you all over, Treasure."

He unbuttoned each button as he kissed the hollow of her neck. Treasure arched her body in response to his touch, which made his dick even harder. He ground into her hips to relieve some of the tension building within him as he slid her white lacey bra away to gain access to her breasts. He ripped his lips from her neck to lick the areola around each breast.

"Takoda—"

Her voice broke when he took her nipple in his mouth and bit down gently on her nipple. She gasped out a moan.

"I need you inside me."

"You'll have me, baby, but not before I fuck that pussy of yours with my mouth." He said while sliding his palm down the center of her sex.

She arched her lower back into his palm, and that was all he needed to slide her jeggings and panties down her thighs and begin pressing his tongue into her inner seam. She was already wet with need and tasted like vanilla and butterscotch as his tongue plunged in and out of her. Her back arched again as she fisted his hair and let out a low growl.

"Oh baby, I can't, I—"

He plunged two fingers inside her pussy as his tongue circled her clit.

"You can. Come for me, baby. I want to hear you scream my name."

Her slick inner folds pulsated and clamped around his fingers as if performing on cue to his command.

"Takoda!"

Her voice was husky and wild, and he loved how his name sounded while he made her come.

"Good, girl. That's it. Keep coming for me, baby."

He continued to plunge his fingers in and out of her until the last waves of her orgasm faded. And that's when thoughts of Nayati hit him like a Mac truck.

FUCK! We shouldn't be doing this. What have I done?

He quickly pulled her towards his chest as he started redressing her.

"Treasure? Baby," He cupped her cheek before continuing, "You still belong to Nayati. Even if we want things to be different, I still have no right to claim you. I shouldn't have let this happen."

Every word he spoke shattered him. He wanted to make Treasure his. So much so that it hurt to breathe another word about Nayati and the stupid situation he put the two of them in. If it wasn't for shifter law—he'd claim her right here and right now, but he couldn't—not without Nayati's permission. And the worst part of it all was laying witness to her eyes, wet with the sting of rejection. He hadn't seen the same expression since the day they first met.

"It's just he's already upset, and I don't want to make things worse. He's involved the council with all of this. And he is doing that because he wants me out of this territory."

"I don't want that! Stay here in Wyoming, please!" She practically screamed the words, and tears now made a constant stream down her face. "You can't leave me because I can't handle that!"

"I can't leave you, either. It's why I've been fighting this with Nayati for the past six months. But he's set in his ways, and I can't help but wonder if that's because of Lenox's constant meddling."

"No—you don't understand! I'd rather die than live a life without you."

He found it hard to believe what she had said. And part of it was because he was feeling the same way. The thought of her feeling similarly shocked him. His heart pounded heavily in his chest, and it seemed like it would explode. It continued to beat in such a way as if to prove he couldn't be without her. There'd be no way to leave her behind now. Not when they were becoming this close. He'd soon become her Alpha—that is what he hoped because that was what was agreed upon so long ago. At least, that was how all of this was supposed to be.

"Takoda, I never took on a mate in Nayati's pack because I always knew that my heart belonged to you. Even when I first met you, I just knew I'd one day be yours. It was the sole reason I didn't flee from the cave you discovered me in. At first, I thought my feelings stemmed from being promised to your pride. I was grateful that you took me in since I had nowhere else to go. But now that I'm older, I've become more attached to you. Our bond is growing. Don't you agree? I mean, I was daydreaming about kissing you tonight." She said as she buried her head in his chest.

"I understand you may not want me to leave, Treasure. I don't either. Wyoming is my home. But Nayati isn't leaving me with many choices. He's been trying to pick a fight with me for the past six months. And I refuse to engage. If I do, I will lose my best friend." He said as he lifted her chin with his index finger and deepened his gaze upon her.

"I get it. You've been friends for such a long time." She quickly pulled away from him and lowered her gaze.

His eyebrows knitted.

"No, I didn't mean Nayati, Treasure. Yes, he has been a friend, but I meant you. I don't want to lose you if I go against Nayati. There's no way I'd fight him—not when you are still in his pack. Because I don't want you getting hurt. I'd rather die."

"Don't say that either!" She said as she pounded

his chest with her fist. Her tears glistened in the moonlight and left a large, wet pool on the top portion of his bare chest. "I can't lose you, Takoda. I can't."

She buried her head in his shoulder and continued to sob uncontrollably. Takoda wrapped his arms around her and kissed the top of her head. He wanted nothing more than to take her pain away. None of Nayati's actions made sense. He held her tighter. But it was impossible to console her.

"Baby, why all the tears?" He asked, even though he already knew the answer.

"I want to be with you. The more time I spend with you, the more I realize you are my mate. This isn't about lust with me." She said as she swallowed hard and pulled away from him. "I'm sorry. I shouldn't have said anything, but I can't keep this to myself anymore. Ever since I met you, I've known that you are my fated mate, Takoda. If Nayati wants to pick a fight with you and your pride," her voice trailed slightly before continuing, "I can't be a part of it. You all mean too much to me. I'd leave first. I couldn't hurt you or any of the pride. All of you took me in. How could he even fathom harming any of you?"

"You think we are fated mates?" His eyes searched hers as he palmed her shoulders.

It's not like that idea didn't cross his mind on more than one occasion while he'd been with her in the last six months, but he had no idea she perceived the same.

"I shouldn't have said anything. Really, I shouldn't have. I'm sorry. Just understand that if this rift comes down to another Civil Were War, I will go rogue and leave Wyoming myself. I get you can't leave your pride because you have to protect them. But I'd rather leave than hurt any of you."

He cupped her cheeks.

"We will figure out something. I promise. But for now, let's finish getting dressed and grab a bite to eat." He said in a silky tone while stroking her cheeks with his thumbs and wiping the tears that stained her face.

"Promise?" She said as she pressed her cheek into his right palm. "Because I'm pretty sure I can't live without you. I am certain that would break me."

"I can't lie. It'd gut me too if I'd have to live without you. It's safe to say that I'm falling for you."

She smiled and palmed his hands that were still on her cheeks.

"I love you, too, Takoda."

ONCE THEY WERE DRESSED, Takoda wrapped his arm around Treasure. The pair headed towards his car from the thick of the forest near his side of the Wyoming compound territory.

"Where would you like to go?" He asked as he opened the passenger's side of his Nightfall Mica colored Lexus LS.

"I'm the wrong person to ask. Nayati hasn't really let me out of the compound much. This was the first time in forever." She palmed the buttery leather as she slid in.

"When was the last time you went out?" He asked after sliding into the driver's seat and turning on the car, and it purred to attention.

"When you took me to that pizza place?"

"Alibi Pub? That was at least six to eight months ago—maybe more. He hasn't let you out of the compound in that long?"

"No, he hasn't. But let's not talk about him. Let's take this time to enjoy some dinner."

"What do you feel like having?"

"Honestly, pizza with a beer sounds good right about now."

"Well, Alibi, it is then."

It was a short drive down the mountainside to get to the pub. Takoda put his arm around her once they were out of the car and led her in. They sat over at the bar where several Flatscreen TVs were playing various baseball and soccer games. The bartender came over and placed a napkin in front of them as they were getting into their seats.

"What can I get you?"

Treasure scanned the draft beers quickly and smiled.

"I'll have the Pakos IPA."

"Certainly. And for you, sir?"

"The Easy Street Wheat, please."

"Alright. coming right up." The bartender said as he grabbed two chilled mugs from the freezer and poured the beer. He quickly returned and placed them both on the cocktail napkins. "Would you like a menu?"

Takoda looked at Treasure.

"I'm fine with a Margherita pizza. I'm not all that fancy. Cheese is good for me."

"A purist. I like it." He turned to the server, "The Margherita pizza, please."

"Wonderful choice." The bartender said, grabbing the menus from their hands. He then went over to the cash register to type in their order.

"So, about earlier," Takoda cleared his throat before he started, "I didn't mean to hurt you. I just don't want to do anything that could put you in danger. You are important to me, Treasure. Very important."

He branded a half-smile in her direction, but she lowered her eyes in retort.

"Takoda, I was serious earlier. If Nayati wants to pick a fight, I will go rogue and leave Wyoming. I'm not fighting Nayati's craziness, nor do I wish to help contribute to another Civil Were War."

"But that's if you can escape. The laws are quite clear. If Lenox—"

"I'm well aware of the laws. If he announces the fight before I've had the chance to announce my going rogue, I will have no choice but to fight. Unless—" her voice trailed.

Takoda's brows knitted.

"I've already told you, marking you as mine is too risky. That will most definitely send Nayati over the edge."

"It's not risky, according to the gods or the council."

"True. No one can deny a chosen mate. However, there are the laws of betrayal to think about, too. Those are also clear," Takoda said as he placed a hand on her thigh. "He could kill you." He pressed circles onto her exposed skin right above her knee as he continued. "I can't be in a world without you. I love you too much."

He screwed his eyes shut and let out a breath.

"If only I wasn't so protective of you. And if only I wasn't such a stickler for the laws, I could have taken you into the fold sooner. I worried about my Omegas hurting you, too."

She cupped his hand that was on her thigh.

"Takoda, your thoughtfulness about law and how you rule as Alpha over the pride is one reason I fell in love with you in the first place. Besides, even if you weren't such a stickler, your pride is. No Omega would have taken me seriously a year and a half ago because I wasn't a full-fledged adult back then. All you would have been doing in that amount of time was stopping the fights amongst them since they all want to be the luna—you know that."

He let out a long breath, kissed her cheek, and pressed his head against her forehead.

"You are right. And I did all of this to protect you, but this abundance of caution seems to be biting me in the ass. The gods are toying with us. Allowing us and our cougars to know we are fated mates and then denying us the blood right to be together."

"It's not fair. It isn't. I understand that, but we have to find a way where we can be together. I can't stay in Nayati's compound for much longer. Not when we both know Lenox is up to something. He's been coming around the compound far too often. Something is wrong. Lenox is up to something big. I can feel it."

Takoda cupped Treasure's cheeks.

"You have no idea how much I want you to be wrong, but I know you are right deep in my gut."

He kissed her forehead and took a pull from his beer. Her eyes glistened in the track lighting, boasting her impossible brown eyes. He found himself getting lost in them as the conversation turned to happier subjects. She told him all about her dreams of becoming a graphic designer. Her parents encouraged her to pursue those dreams. Until Nayati started feuding with him, even Nayati encouraged her to go to college. She wasn't that much younger than he was—only five years. But life hadn't hardened her with its lack-luster yet. He saw that as she continued to talk about projects, she'd already done in design and how many more she still wanted to do.

THREE

They finished their pizza and drafts within a scant hour. Being careful not to bust a curfew for Treasure, they headed to the car shortly after paying the bill.

"We should head back, so Nayati doesn't get suspicious," Takoda said as he opened the car door for Treasure. "The thing is, I don't want the night to end just yet."

His lips were a breath from hers as her body pressed against the car.

"What did you have in mind?" Treasure said with a teasing chuckle as her palm brushed Takoda's extended arm that was still holding the car door.

"This."

He crashed his lips onto hers, and electric heat rushed through her as she wrapped her arms around him. In fear of none of this being real, she opened her eyes to see his face. That's when she saw Nayati come up from behind the densely wooded area surrounding them, heading for Takoda's car.

"I allow you the privilege of trust, and this is how you repay me, Treasure?"

His voice was dark, his eyes wild with hatred as he spat out the words.

"Nayati, brother, it is not what you think."

Takoda whipped around on his heel with outstretched palms as if to signify a truce. Nayati shot a disdainful look in Takoda's direction.

"Do not call me your brother. Brothers do not betray one another, and neither does an Omega of my pack." He then turned to Treasure. "As your Alpha, I forbid you to see anyone outside of the compound from this day forward. I can't trust you. Therefore I will confine you to a room of my choosing in the compound from here on out until you learn obedience. Do I make myself clear?"

Nayati grabbed Treasure's arm and yanked her into the woods before Takoda, or she had a chance to protest. Treasure screamed and tried to break free from Nayati's grasp as Nayati pulled her further and further into the wooded area.

Takoda shot after them and was at their heels. He tried to reach for Treasure as he began to shift into his cougar. But before he had the chance, four of Nayati's pride jumped out from the dark shadows of the forest and surrounded Takoda.

"Takoda!"

"I'm coming, Treasure!"

The four closed in on Takoda, snarling and snapping at him. One lunged for his throat, and the other three forced him to his knees.

"You will never have her. Never! You understand me?" said the one whose fingers were tightly wrapped around Takoda's throat. Takoda struggled with the shifter's hands, and then another one from behind him knocked him over the head. Takoda's knees buckled, and he fell to the ground. The smell of soil mixed with copper filled his nostrils as the four of them continued to beat on him. Takoda struggled to gain the upper hand, but try as he might, he could not coax his cougar to come out. Not when the four of them were in human form. It was the law. No shifter could shift into their animal unless provoked by one who has already shifted.

He could not understand why this was happening right now. Why wasn't Nayati's pride being more aggressive? Why was he having such an issue escaping from them while they were in their human form? And why couldn't his cougar be coaxed to come out—even if it was for self-preservation?

Takoda had heard of other shifters having problems with releasing their animal side. Still, those were always halves—they weren't born with the innate skill like he was. Something was wrong, terribly wrong. He continued to block each kick, punch, and bite, but his eyes grew heavy within a few more moments.

"Takoda! No! Don't hurt him!"

The words kept ringing in his ears, and he tried to struggle with his mind to keep himself conscious. He needed to save Treasure—now more than ever. As the kicks and punches seemed to dull in the severity of pain, he knew he'd blackout soon. Takoda could only think of how he should have claimed her while they were in the forest earlier. None of this would be happening right now if he claimed Treasure as his mate. All of this was his fault from the very beginning.

The last thing his eyes fixed on before everything went black was how tightly Nayati's grip was on Treasure. The man had no right to hurt her like that as he led her further into the woods towards their pride's compound.

TAKODA AWOKE and found himself back at his own compound with a fire burning in his fireplace and a blanket wrapped around him. He palmed his forehead as a rush of pain came over him.

What happened? The last thing I remembered?

A rush of the evening's events came over him.

Oh, no! Treasure!

He shot up from his lying position on the couch. That was a bad idea since a sudden rush of pain hit him from what seemed like his entire body all at once. He let out a whimper.

"Fuck!"

"Careful, Takoda! You took a pretty bad beating! Lay back and drink some tea. The boys and I found you, and just in time, too. You had lost a lot of blood. What happened?"

Takoda let out a breath that he didn't realize he was holding in. "He took Treasure." He let out another breath that was followed by a sigh. "I don't understand it, Viho. Why would Nayati renege on his promise to me? This goes beyond his quarrel with me. If I didn't know any better, I'd think he's doing it to keep Treasure as his own Omega concubine."

"Honestly, Takoda, I wouldn't put anything past the man at this point. I've been worried about him just as long as you, and I think it's time we either take the fight to him. I don't see us getting out of this any other way. Unless we leave Wyoming."

"You get that I trust you with my life, Viho. Despite everything you've been through, you chose to be my Beta instead of Nayati's, and I can never thank you enough for that loyalty and trust. But you are Cheyenne, and according to current council law, you have rights to this land. Not to mention the fact that you are blood-related to some of the Omegas in

Nayati's pack. I can't ask you to fight alongside me. That'd be wrong of me."

"Don't go soft on me! Stop it with this crap! I am in your pride because I wanted to be. And I go where this pride needs me. You are my Alpha, and I will do as you wish, but if your wish is for me to side with Nayati, I'm afraid I cannot fulfill that wish for you. He's changed. We both get that, and the longer we stay here, the longer we keep this pride in danger." Viho said as he passed some herbal smelling tea to Takoda. "I understand you love her, and I, like you, sense that she is your fated mate and our pride's Luna Queen. But we must think of the entire pride's safety—first and foremost. I'm sorry, my Alpha, but you know I am right."

"Yes, I do, and the decision is simple. The pride must leave Wyoming for safety. Take the pride with you and protect them."

"You are not coming with us?" Viho said with widened eyes.

"Not when he still has her."

"You can't fight his pride alone. That's suicide!" Viho said with knitted brows.

"He's not alone. He has me." A voice projected from the kitchen.

Viho peered in the general direction of the voice, and Donovan appeared
through the threshold.

"Donovan, forgive me. I understand you are a

powerful Alpha in your own right, but it's just the two of you against his fleet of Omegas."

Donovan patted Viho on the shoulder.

"We will do just fine, especially when the pride and my Sonya are safely away from Wyoming. Once the battle ends, or gods willing, we come to a truce—we will send for you all. But honestly? I'm hoping we won't need to fight. I'm hoping we can drive a wedge between Nayati and Lenox. That's the key to solving this entire problem."

"My Alpha, I beg of you to let me stay here with you so I can aid you in your fight with Nayati."

"No, Viho. You must lead our pride to safety. Should we not be successful, you will become our pride's Alpha. And that is a direct order. You have no choice but to obey me."

"Yes, Alpha, I understand." Viho nodded. "I don't like it, but I will prepare the pride to leave at dusk."

"Very good," Takoda said as he patted Viho on the shoulder once more. "I am certain you will not let me down."

Viho got up from the couch and walked towards the front door in a slouch, signifying defeat.

"Do you honestly think we've got a snowball's chance in hell of breaking into that compound and rescuing Treasure without alerting Nayati?" Donovan asked Takoda.

"No. Lenox has a sixth sense. We are psychically

connected—it's why we've always called each other brother. So the second I set foot in his territory, he'd be alerted to me coming. This will more than less likely be a bloody battle if you ask me. And that's honestly fine by me because I want to pummel him for hurting her."

"I figured this wouldn't be easy, but maybe we should focus on Lenox? He's the real reason all of this is happening."

"Donovan, this is not your fight. I will understand if—"

"The fuck it isn't! He wants me out, too—or did you forget that? I'm not backing down from this fight. Especially since the last time he pulled shit like this, he started The Civil Were War. As far as I'm concerned, this ends here in Wyoming because he is the sole reason that you and I have had to fight to protect who we love. Now, his ancestors may have once lived off of this land, but Lenox forgets a pack was here long before he set foot on these mountains. And might I remind you they are mountains both you and I welcomed him to? Our packs and prides all used to coexist together well before Lenox came around to cause trouble. This is Lenox's third strike. We have no choice but to take him down. If he wants war, then it's now a full-on fight that he's gonna get!"

"In all the squabbles over the past six months, I almost forgot about him and how he caused The

Civil Were War. I'm not even sure how I could forget since I was there fighting alongside you and Nayati."

"I didn't," Donovan said with a dark chuckle.

"Yeah, listen, for all it is worth, I'm sorry I got you into this mess. I should have never pushed you to allow Lenox to stay here in the mountains, to begin with. It was a stupid idea, but I thought he'd be harmless since he lost so many of his recruits. Of course, having some members of the council who are blood-related to members of his pack back east made it more difficult. Once the council overruled my wishes, it was out of our hands."

Donovan shook his head.

"It's not your fault. The fact is, it had been a couple of years, and, like you and the council, I thought Lenox had changed. So that makes us all in this same messy boat." Donovan said as he patted Takoda's shoulder. "Let's just make sure that you and I wipe the floor clean—if you catch my drift. I'm not ready to die, and I know you aren't either. But before we do this, I need to ask you a favor, my friend."

"Of course! Anything!"

"Please see to it that Sonya goes with your pride. I'd never forgive myself if anything were to happen to her while we fight Lenox and Nayati."

Takoda clasped Donovan's forearm with the palm of his hand and gave it a good shake.

"Consider it done, my friend. I will let my right

hand know to take her kicking and screaming if he has to. Care to join me in a smoke?" Takoda asked as he pulled out a peace pipe that was wrapped in ivory-colored leather and had a turquoise bear carved on the end to hold the tobacco. He pinched in some kinnikinnick into the circular bowl and then lit it up. Rings of smoke intermixed with the swirls of smoke coming from the fireplace.

"I'd love to. It's been a long time since I've been invited into a sacred circle. Being rogue, I haven't been with a pack in a long time."

"What made you want to come to Wyoming, anyway? I mean, there was like a population of one when you first settled in the town that you're in—Buford—right?"

Donovan shrugged his shoulders.

"Didn't trust myself around humans. Ocean didn't exactly take me under her wing once she bit me. I mean—not that I left her a choice, of course, and I basically broke up with her the instant she broke my skin with her bite. It wasn't until a few days later that I realized what I had become."

"You," Takoda's voice trailed for a moment before continuing, "you were human?"

"Yes. Why are you so surprised?" Donovan said with a raised brow.

"Because no half has the strength to control their shifter side as you've done. It can take decades for a pup to grasp its powers fully. That's why many introduced through a bite have been trained by Zhang. But you—you weren't trained by him? How do you do it? You've been so in control since I've known you."

"Yeah, well, Ocean wasn't exactly a garden variety werewolf either."

"She's a dire."

"Yeah, she's a dire, alright—but you knew that. Anyway, all I know is I wanted nothing to do with her or humans after she bit me. Of course, Sonya changed my mind on all of that." Donovan said with a smile.

"The dire explains a lot. It's rare, but a dire can pass their traits onto the ones they've bitten on occasion. Since she wanted to claim you as her mate, I'm sure it was easier for her to transfer her powers. Can I ask you something? I mean, you can totally not answer if it's too personal."

"Spill it, Takoda."

"Did you know right from the start that Sonya was your mate?"

"I wouldn't say within the first minute or anything like that, but yeah. On the first day of meeting her, I knew that something was different about her. My wolf did, too. Why are you asking me this? Is it because the perpetual bachelor has finally found Treasure as someone to tame those unruly wonton ways of yours?" Donovan said as he palmed his chest for a dramatic effect before letting out a hearty chuckle.

"Stop!" Takoda said with a chuckle. "But—yeah. I guess she always has had a pull on me. The thing is, I didn't realize it until now. Sure, my cougar always wanted to protect her, but my human side only saw her as a kid for the past year."

Donovan shrugged.

"We don't get to choose, really, man. It's fate. Fate—like shit—happens." Donovan said with another chuckle before continuing. "Like you, I really thought no woman would get on my radar. I was too busy shielding them all from the monster I'd become."

"But I was born a shifter. There's a difference there."

"I get that. And that gave you an advantage in taming that cougar of yours—something I never thought I had."

"Not from where I'm sitting," Takoda said as he took in a long drag from the pipe before handing it over to Donovan. "To me, you are a natural-born shifter. It's in your blood. I'm telling ya—I've never seen a newb as in control as you are."

"Is that so?" Donovan also took a long drag from the pipe and then passed it back to Takoda.

"Even if she wasn't a dire, there's another explanation for all of this. Some people are born shifters and don't have the capability to shift. I suspect that might be what happened to you, and you just weren't aware of it."

"Wait, this makes sense. We believe that happened to Sonya."

"Yes. And that might also explain why it was so easy for you to reject Ocean as your fated mate. No newb can't resist a queen—even Alphas have a hard time with that unless they are born into the role."

"I recall Morgan rejected Keme," Donovan said as he shrugged his shoulders before continuing. "Wasn't that a similar thing? The packs in the northeast talked a lot when we were preparing for The Civil Were War. Who knew giving Dante a little alcohol would loosen his lips?" Donovan said with a chuckle. "But did that have more to do with Morgan or Arizona?"

"Probably a little of both. Morgan is a werewitch dire and was Alec's soulmate in a prior lifetime. That's a powerful lineage. But Chepi, being the Alpha chief of her tribal pride, also is a strong lineage. Personally? I think the gods had their hands in both of those unions—not just with Alec and Morgan."

"Yeah, um, shit like this makes my head spin. It's hard enough navigating through this lifetime, so perhaps I'll just quit while I'm ahead. I'm merely bringing it up because Ocean wasn't my fated mate. It could be as simple as that, too."

"Well, it's not that simple. Remember, we all

have free will. We shifters don't have to choose the same partner throughout every lifetime. With witches, it gets more complicated, but even they have a bit of leeway with the gods."

"I always wondered why Raine and Skye found each other in every lifetime they have reincarnated into. Guess that's no mystery anymore." Donovan said as he shrugged his shoulders.

"They have an epic love that's not much different from fated mates," Takoda said as he took another puff from the pipe before continuing. "What if we fail, Donovan? What if I lose her?"

"Let's not think about that right now. Plus? It might not come to that. Like I said—we can either try to pin Nayati against Lenox, or we devise a brilliant plan to bust her out of there undetected, and no one will get hurt."

"This is true. It could happen, I guess. But we'd need a layout of the land. Does anyone happen to have the blueprints of his compound lying around somewhere?" Takoda said with a chuckle.

"As a matter of fact, I do, but they're at the house. I'll stop by first thing tomorrow morning, and we can look for weak points to enter his compound undetected. Then tomorrow night, I'll bring my night vision cameras, and we can look for areas less guarded by the Omegas. It'd be ideal if an entrance had little to no guards."

"Perfect."

They took the last few puffs from the peace pipe as the embers disappeared from the dying fire in the fireplace. Donovan got to his feet.

"Get some rest, so those bones of yours recover," Donovan said as he opened the front door to leave Takoda's place.

"Will do, my friend."

Takoda paced back and forth in his living room with a cup of coffee in his hand. He was so deep in thought he really didn't realize he might wear out the floor with his pacing. But this was something he couldn't help. He needed to get Treasure away from Nayati. Nothing else was more important to him. Not even his own safety mattered.

He tossed and turned most of the night, going over every likely scenario to get Treasure out of there undetected. Many of the plans that he came up with had too many flaws. But a handful of them proved promising enough to him where they might work. He wasn't sure because they relied heavily on the forest and hiding until they found Treasure. As the minutes hardly budged on his microwave clock, he grew anxious for Donovan's arrival so he could run them by the guy. Once he was about to start on cup number four of coffee, he heard Donovan knocking at the door. Takoda opened it to see Donovan sporting an enormous smile on his face.

"There's a great way to get into the complex undetected on this map. Since it's a national forest that leads to his compound, I'm hoping that it's not heavily guarded."

He laid the map out on the coffee table and pointed at the forest area on the map.

"It's butted up against the mountains here. We should be able to get in and probably out with no problem."

"I never noticed that he was so close to the national forest before."

"Me neither. It's better to wait till nightfall, and then we can scout this pathway out before getting Treasure. Being the photographer I am, I have plenty of night vision cameras we can work with."

"My guess is that he's keeping her in the main office building area of the compound," Takoda said as he pointed to one building on the map. "There's always one house where they have pride meetings held. It would also be the one place with a room they can hold someone in. I've never had to detain any of the members of my pride. They were all born shifters, so there was no need. Nayati had to, once, though. It was a newly bitten shifter struggling with his new powers. He had trouble controlling himself the first time he shifted—I think his name was Lorring. I had to help Nayati bring that shifter to the lockup area because he was a pretty strong wolf—would have been easier if he was a cougar."

"I can't say that I can relate to his situation because I moved here out of fear of losing it. But I can sympathize with Lorring. Was he better after that first time?"

"We had to call in Zhang—but yeah."

"Well, that's probably a good thing. That old man knows what he is doing. I learned a lot from him when he was helping us fight Lenox last year."

"Indeed. I mean, Zhang tamed Keme—so he can tame any shifter."

"No wonder the council appointed him as the shifter trainer for both the Americas."

The two sat and made idle small talk over a couple of beers until the sun lowered on the horizon, dipping down into the trees. Once dusk turned into nightfall, they packed up Donovan's night vision cameras. Then they headed out of Takoda's place and toward Nayati's.

"I don't think it's a good idea to shift. If Nayati's pack sees us, they will take our shifting as a threat." Donovan said as he slung his backpack over his shoulder. "In fact, I'm going to hide the night vision cameras until we absolutely need them because the last thing we need is for them to think we are spying on them, too. That would be an act of war in and of itself."

"Agreed. We can't risk them moving Treasure because we may never find her after that."

"I will not let that happen. If we can avoid a war —I'd rather do that. But getting Treasure out will not be so easy."

"No, you are right, and once she is out, Nayati will gun for me." Said Takoda.

"Let's hope we can convince him otherwise, my friend," Donovan said as he patted Takoda on his shoulder.

The forest was thicker than Takoda remembered. Part of it had to do with the fact that he was hiking in human form—something he rarely does these days. It was just so much easier to hunt the woods in his cougar form. To run through the trees with the wind bristling through his thick, reddish-tawny coat gave him a sense of freedom. He knew he didn't have with any of the females of his pride. The Omegas fawned over him constantly. All of them wanting their piece of his crown. And not only did Takoda have no feelings other than protecting his people. But he also wanted nothing to do with the Omegas that thought of him as nothing more than a change in status.

In all of his years of being a born shifter, he never felt like the prey until he came of age, and the females wanted the prestige of being the pride's luna queen. Not one of them loved him. Which suited him just fine since the feeling was mutual. But the thing that bugged him is that he would have set his feelings aside and called one of them the queen of his pride—at least at one point in his life. It wasn't uncommon for a leader of their pride to take on a mate just for the people. His grandfather had done so. But none of the Omegas vying for the position of luna queen understood the responsibility of being one.

To wield any kind of power means that it comes with responsibility. Takoda knew that firsthand when his father groomed him to become the Alpha. But these girls didn't know the first thing about being a queen. They all thought of the position as sipping tea and eating crumpets. The title of a queen of a shifter pride was far more complicated than the human dignitaries. Sure, the humans had conflicts when in power, but commoners thought they mostly threw charity balls.

The title of a luna queen was hard work. The woman had to be an influential leader—if not a naturally born one. And Takoda didn't have the time or the patience to make them understand that with the title comes the responsibility of protecting and providing for the entire pride in his absence. His mother would have been more than willing to train any woman he wanted to have as his mate, but she died too early in his adolescence to teach anyone.

Any woman he took on now as his mate would be his responsibility alone to train to fight in his absence. Even if his father was still alive, it wasn't the former Alpha's job to prepare a would-be queen. No. That responsibility laid squarely on his shoulders, and it was part of why he'd been procrastinating taking on a mate.

A memory of discovering Treasure in that cave so many years ago rushed through his mind as he passed some thick brush.

I can't survive on my own. I'm not strong enough.

The words stung him then. They were full of innocence, full of fear. He wondered if those same thoughts were running through Treasure's mind now, as she was no doubt being beaten and held against her will. The two things he tried to protect her from with his Omegas. He wanted to pummel Nayati for all of this getting out of hand, but he couldn't. Deep down, he knew all of this was Lenox, and the thought that he had failed her shattered him.

Most women in his pride were fearful of another civil war among the shifters. None of them fought by his side, nor did they take on the responsibilities of hunting for the pride. They all took care of the children and the elders. Takoda, Nayati, and a few of the other Beta warriors protected the parameters and fought in the war by his side.

If stealing Treasure back would cause enough

unrest where Nayati declares war, so be it. Takoda was more and more prepared to go up against his old friend, Nayati, the closer they came to his compound. He wouldn't fail his Treasure this time around by being complaisant. He'd fight for her and her rights as a shifter—even if it meant that the pride must leave Wyoming. Takoda knew it was something she didn't want for him, and she was prepared to go rogue, but he wouldn't let her do that. Not when it was clear she was his.

FIVE

The sound of Nayati slapping Treasure's cheek clapped through the central area of the community house of the compound. It echoed into the depths of every corner of the tiny room he had her prisoner in.

"You will obey me, Omega, because I am your Alpha—not Takoda! Do you understand me?"

Nayati spat the words out to her as he tightened the shackles he had around Treasure's wrists. He hoisted her up onto the tips of her toes in the middle of a small room she knew as the dungeon. It was where they housed any pride that couldn't control themselves when they first came into their powers. Nayati used the room only once when a cougar they took in as a rogue from the Civil Were War shifted every time he got angry.

That was the only time she had seen Nayati use

it before Lenox came to stay in Wyoming. But within the past six months, Nayati used it more and more to gain control over the members of his pride that were doubting his orders. And he performed all of this submission in Lenox's presence, which was why she wasn't surprised to see Lenox at Nayati's right just outside the room's doorway.

She feared this room because of how many Omegas Nayati broke into submission. The pride members who were unlucky to come into this room eventually learned to seek permission for everything, including the ability to shift. It was sad to see their will ripped from them because of Lenox's suggestive tyrannic rule.

The act seemed like something barbaric to her. Her former Alpha and father would have never done such a thing. Then again, everyone in their pride was born a shifter. They were fully aware of their animal side, so she couldn't be sure what her father would do if he was forced to help a newly bitten shifter control their urges. But she knew in her heart that it wouldn't be anything like what Lenox was doing. One of the first things that drew her to Takoda was him not having holding cells in his compound as Nayati did.

Takoda's pride was like her old pride—they respected one another and taught each shifter how to come into their own well before that first shift came over them. It was what Jacy Black, her father, believed in. Nayati used to be the same. But now that Lenox was running Nayati's pride, everything changed.

Another sharp sting came upon her cheek.

"You will also look at me when I talk to you, Omega! I expect to be treated with the respect I deserve as your Alpha. You do not belong to Takoda. You belong to me, and you will remain in this compound bound to me as I see fit."

His tone disgusted her, and so did his breath, making her even more complacent about his demands. Her body began to vibrate, starting within her gut, and continued to pulse out through to her extremities. She had felt this sensation once before, and it was the day her father, the Alpha of her pride, died in battle. She remembered her father explaining the phenomenon when she was a tiny kitten, and the war wasn't even a thought in any shifter's mind.

He explained it comes over every shifter born to lead a tribal pride of their own. However, when Treasure lost her entire pride during the Civil Were War, there was no one for her to lead. And before Takoda discovered her, the thought of going rogue terrified her because she was only 17. She had no idea how to hunt or provide for herself. It was the only reason she agreed to have Nayati take her as part of his pride until Takoda welcomed her into his own fold as a full-fledged adult.

The vibration, the one her father, Jacy Black, explained as The Bourgeoning, humming inside of her, stirred something in her she never thought she had the power to do. A great power welled within her rigid muscles, allowing her to resist the Alpha currently slapping her in the face. Treasure locked her eyes on Nayati and spat in his face as soon as he came within close enough range. She knew that would earn her another slap from the man, but it was worth it as far as she was concerned.

"You are not—nor will you ever be my Alpha!" Her eyes narrowed as she gave him a smug grin.

Nayati slapped her again, but this time harder. Heat radiated from her cheek as if a bruise formed the instant his hand left her face.

"You will learn to bow down to me eventually," Nayati said as he wrapped his hand around her throat.

Treasure still had her eyes locked on his. She refused to glance away, and she refused to show weakness in her voice from his grip.

"I'm unbreakable, bastard." She shot another smug grin in Nayati's direction.

"You should take heed." Lenox stepped into the room before continuing. "He's very good at making Omegas submit like the bitches they are."

He leaned into her ear, and his breath was as cold as the words he formed.

Nayati released his grip from Treasure's throat

and slapped the side of her face again. Something sticky and wet rolled down her chin from the corner of her lip. And from the copper scent that now permeated the room, Treasure could assume that Nayati broke the skin with complete certainty.

"Scout Kimana, guard this door and ensure the Omegas do not allow this traitor to her people to eat. She's only allowed water until further notice." Nayati barked as he backed away from Treasure.

"Yes, my Alpha." Said Kimana as she bowed her head to him.

They all left the tiny cubical of a room and slammed the door on Treasure. The bang echoed through the small chamber. The echo reminded her of the sharp change that had built up within Nayati for the past six months. Not one ounce of warmth remained in the hollowed eyes that glared at her for the past half-hour he was beating her. Nothing about him reminded her of the caring person he once was to her when he took her into the tribal pride.

All was wonderful until Lenox came. Nayati's attitude towards his people, Takoda, and what she was to Takoda had changed on a dime. All of it turned to shit the minute Lenox became an elder of their pride. At any other point in shifter history, no werewolf would have been accepted into a cougar pride—let alone become an Elder of one. Still, the Civil Were War had changed every shifter's history.

Prides and packs were decimated. And the only way to gain strength in numbers was to break the 14th Century Peace Treaty Common Trifecta Law and allow all the shifters to become one sizeable and a proverbial melting pot of a race.

In theory, there wasn't much of a foreseeable problem with that. Especially when Alphas, lunas, Betas, and Deltas all agreed to train any rogue that they came across during war recovery efforts. The rogue was to become an Omega of their tribe and would only ascend in the pack or pride if the Alpha saw fit. A sorcerer known for founding the initial treaty in the 14th century lived out the second half of his life in New England. He was called Zhang. And according to the legends that Nayati told her, Zhang agreed to teach the shifter community how to train newbies. This way, they would be less threatening to the magical community once the war was over.

Zhang helped eradicate the old treaty because he had the respect of the shifters for creating it in the first place. Magic back then was far less under-stood. Any mixing of magical races was prohibited under the law. No shifter or witch could marry a vampire. Such a union was punishable by death because there was fear that the child would become an abomination. Lenox used The Common Trifecta Law as an excuse for waging The Civil Were War against any shifter who blessed the union of Alec, the King of the Vlad Vampire Clan, and Morgan, a dire werewitch. They cast no spell for the pregnancy to occur. She became pregnant as the result of a gift from the gods. Once that was determined, the war ended, and now, with the advancement of culture and thanks to Zhang, shifters had a better grasp of magical powers. The rest of the magical community considered shifters the most barbaric out of any magical race. But no one saw this coming.

Not one part of the old or now new treaty helped with Lenox's betrayal of council law. At first, she was in the dark, like Takoda. She just thought that Nayati was becoming as power-hungry as the werewolf Alpha, Lenox. But now that she was a prisoner in her own caretaker's pride, she knew the truth. Lenox appeared to have learned more than just a spell to reverse his son's magic. And certainly more than the blood oath he used to create an army large enough to start The Civil Were War. He now had another way to compel Nayati and the elders to do his bidding.

Lenox was always at Nayati's side—no matter what the task was in the pride. Lenox was there even for something as trivial as her being locked up. And now that they had shackled her, she realized Lenox was never without his staff. At first, Treasure assumed it was just a walking stick, but once Lenox leaned into her ear, she could get a closer look at it. The thing contained red feathers, the shell of a small turtle, and bones from what appeared to be a small animal in nature at the top of the stick. This combination only meant one thing—the walking stick wasn't just something to aid him in movement. It was a shaman staff.

Most shifters, especially werewitches, used shamanic magic for healing. But in Lenox's case, it was more than less likely used for the dark arts. The war alone convinced her the staff was to blame for Nayati's complete 180. She had to figure out a way to escape her cubical confines, find the staff, and destroy it.

Another vibration hummed through her body. But this one differed from the first. It was warm, comforting, and protective. Her eyes widened the minute her brain connected the feelings with the person she always experienced them with.

Takoda!

She sensed his essence approaching the compound, and a pang hit her gut as her heart pounded out of her chest. Beads of sweat formed on her back, and the cool night air made her shiver as she came to a deadly realization. If she could sense his presence, Nayati most likely did too, and that horrified her. She was grateful that Takoda was coming for her, but it would kill her if anything happened to him. For the first time in her life, her heart tugged for another. She needed to protect him from Nayati and the spell he was under.

Treasure looked at the shackles they had put her

in, and they appeared to be magical in nature, which meant only one thing. She wouldn't be able to shift to get out of them. Thankfully, the gods blessed her with small wrists. If she could make her thumbs tighten into her palm enough, she'd be able to escape the shackles. Then cause a diversion with the pocket lighter and herbal leaves she'd always carried. Treasure was like a boy scout. She always brought one along with sage and bay leaves if she ever needed to perform an emergency smudging. Burning the combination could sedate the guard long enough to escape before Takoda set foot in the compound.

She quickly tightened her thumbs into her palms, and within a few quick moments, she freed herself from the shackles. Treasure then fumbled around in her jean pockets and pulled out the sage, bay leaves, and the lighter. She lit one end of a large bay and sage leaf combination and fanned the smoke underneath the crack in the door. After burning five or six leaves in rapid succession, she heard a loud thud, signifying the guard was thoroughly sedated. She slowly opened the door and saw the guard out cold. Treasure tiptoed over the guard's body and peered around the corner into the hallway. Surprisingly, no one else was in the main compound. She quickly when out the door and snuck into the shadows to avoid being seen.

After she double-timed it into the thick brush of

the forest, she let out a breath she'd been holding in for what seemed like forever.

Now I just have to find Takoda!

She closed her eyes to concentrate on his presence and sucked in a deep breath. Once her mind was clear enough, a faint hint of Italian bergamot and Sichuan pepper hit her nose.

Takoda!

She immediately shifted into her cougar form and followed the scent for several miles until she came upon a clearing. The cologne was distinct, but all she could see from her vantage point was a man unfamiliar to her. She sensed he was a wolf shifter, so she remained hidden in the shadows until she could determine whether the dark-haired man was a friend or foe.

It, however, seemed odd he was taking pictures at such a late hour in the evening and so close to Nayati's compound. After a few moments of observing the man, Takoda came into view. Her cougar immediately resonated toward his essence, and a hum came over her body once more before she shifted back into her human form.

Takoda looked in the general direction of where she was hiding in the shadows, and Treasure took that as a sign of being able to show herself.

"Takoda!" she hissed in his direction, hoping the louder than normal whisper she uttered wouldn't alert any of Nayati's scouts. They were most likely patrolling the parameter of the compound.

She could see Takoda's head snap towards the large boulder she was hiding behind. His face softened from harsh undertones once she peeked out from behind it.

"Treasure!" He hissed back as he rushed towards her.

His arms wrapped around her before she could take even one step toward him.

"My gods!" He said as he raised her chin towards the moonlight. "I'll rip his heart out for harming you!"

She splayed her palms over his chest and took in his Sauvage scent to calm herself before answering him.

"It's not Nayati's fault, Takoda. I'm now certain of it. He's under some sort of spell. I think Lenox is using the dark arts on Nayati. Some sort of compulsion spell, perhaps? It's got him brainwashed into thinking that we are the enemy. Lenox has this staff—we need to destroy it to break the hold it has on Nayati. And honestly? Now that Lenox has weaseled his way into the elders' tribal council, I believe he has them under his spell, too."

"That would explain why Nayati has done a 180 in six months, and that would also explain the council agreeing to a lot of what Lenox wanted."

Said Donovan as he came over and extended his hand out to Treasure. "Hi. I'm Donovan, I'm a—"

"Wolf-shifter. I have heard of you through Takoda. It's nice to put a face to the name." Treasure said as she took his hand and gave it a shake.

"Well, since we got what we came here for and the introductions are done, can I suggest we leave before they discover she is gone? Once we are back at my place, we can then figure out what to do with all of that staff stuff. I'd say let's go to yours, Takoda, but yours would be the first place Nayati would look for Treasure. And at least with my place, I have the porch where we can see them coming."

"That sounds like a good idea, Donovan." Said Takoda before his eyes fixed back on Treasure. "Can you walk, or do you need me to carry you?"

"I'm okay—really. It looks worse than it is. Once the spell wears off from the shackles they had me in, my rapid healing should kick in."

ONCE THEY REACHED Donovan's place, Takoda turned on a light in the living room.

"Let me get a better look at that bruise on your face."

"Takoda, really—I'm fine."

He peered at her face and then looked at her neck.

"There are bruises on your neck, too? How could he?" His voice trailed slightly before he drew her into his arms. "I won't ever let him hurt you again. I don't care if we must flee to Europe. No one is going to hurt you like this ever again." Takoda's voice grew shakier with each word he uttered.

"Really, babe, I'm okay. I promise."

"This is all my fault. I should've taken you in and right from the start. Then none of this would've ever happened."

She pushed back from him slightly to meet his eyes.

"How can you say that? You couldn't possibly know that Lenox was going to put Nayati under a spell. And you've always told me you didn't take me into your pack because your Omegas would've beaten me."

Takoda cupped her cheeks and pressed his forehead to hers. "I've always had this need to protect you, Treasure."

"I understand, and if his pack hadn't jumped us —I'm sure you and I could've taken him on."

"With all due respect, Treasure, only another Alpha or a Luna could've helped Takoda take them on. Nayati's pride is pretty powerful. And from what I gathered about you through Takoda, you weren't the Alpha of your pack." Said Donovan as he crossed the threshold and closed the door.

"I may not have been the Alpha of the pride, but

I was the daughter of one. Jacy Black was my father." She said as she pulled away from Takoda's embrace.

Donovan and Takoda locked on to her gaze, mouths slightly agape and eyes widening at each word.

"Don't act so surprised! Why would I have told any of you when you first came across me? We were in a Civil Were War. You would've killed me if you found out I had Alpha blood running through my veins. That was the law. So I had no choice but to protect myself by making myself appear weak."

"Okay, I can understand that back then when I had Nayati take you in, but why wait until now to tell me?"

Treasure shrugged her shoulders before responding.

"Honestly, I didn't think about it all that much. I kinda blocked a lot out to preserve my sanity. I'm basically an orphan, and I thought it was normal not to feel an allegiance to Nayati's pride since all he was doing was fostering me. But something strange happened to me when I was in that cell. It's hard to explain—it felt like an energy was coming over me. Kinda like I was gaining new self-confidence or something. I mean, the younger version of me would've been terrified and probably wouldn't have tried to escape on my own. But this electricity that rushed through me gave me the courage to escape."

"The Bourgeoning!" Takoda said with widened eyes.

"What's that? I've never heard of it before." Treasure asked with a knitted brow.

"Well, most packs and prides have established Alphas and Lunas these days—at least around here. There hasn't been a need for the next generation to come into their rightful power because none of the Alphas are old enough to retire. That's why the term is unfamiliar to most." Said Takoda.

"Except till now," Donovan interjected.

Treasure and Takoda's eyebrows knitted at Donovan's response.

"Isn't it obvious to the two of you?" Donovan chuckled as he gestured a hand between the two of them. "She's your Luna, Takoda."

They still had a puzzled look on their faces as they searched Donovan's eyes for clarification.

"Oh, come on! Her father was an Alpha!"

"I still don't think we follow you, Donovan."

"Takoda! If her father was the famous Alpha Jacy Black, that means she has royal blood! And this is our way out of a war with the council and Nayati. Well, once we can break Lenox's spell over Nayati, of course."

"Still not following." Treasure said as she shook her head.

"It's simple. You are a mateless Luna, Treasure. As a royal, you must mate with an available

Alpha—it's in your blood and nature to do so. Therefore, you can't stay in Nayati's pride because he already has a Luna he has mated with. And by law, once a Luna comes into her powers through The Bourgeoning, she must bond with her fated mate by the first full moon. Thankfully, we already know who that fated mate is." Donovan said as he patted Takoda on the shoulder. "The council will have no choice but to accept that you are Takoda's mate and will force Nayati to give you over to Takoda."

"Okay, but Takoda's Shoshone, and I've got Cheyenne blood. How would that help?"

"That's why this solves our problems! What's the one tribe the council recognizes right now in Wyoming?"

Treasure's eyes widened.

"Donovan, you are a genius!"

"I know." He said with a toothy grin. "Now, why don't you both get some sleep? The guest room is just down the hall and to your right. Fresh towels are in the adjoining bathroom, and I'll grab you one of my tees for you to sleep in, Treasure. Think I'll take the first and second watch since you both have some catching up to do." Donovan said with a wink.

Treasure's cheeks flushed, and her eyes immediately darted towards the floor.

"Sorry, Treasure! I'm merely trying to get Takoda's goat. I shouldn't have said anything."

"Fuck you, man. And I mean that is the sincerest way."

"I'm not your type, but clearly she is."

"Dude! That's not cool! Cut that shit out!"

"Sorry, not sorry because I have thin walls, and I know I'll be hearing stuff all night. Try to keep it down—will ya?"

"Donovan! Enough!" Takoda yelled as he led Treasure to the guest room and closed the door behind them.

The last thing on his mind was to make love to her. He knew Donovan was kidding, but it didn't make Takoda feel any better. Though almost fully healed, those bruises still looked painful and were a reminder of what Nayati did to her. He still found it hard to fathom that Nayati hurt her like that. The man didn't have a nasty bone in his body. Which was why he wanted to pummel Lenox—the man that was the real reason behind Treasure's bruises and pain. All Takoda wanted to do was take her in his arms and protect her from everything.

Just barring witness to the bruising made his own face flush with anger. His body shook, and he tried to steady himself as he pressed his palms into the sink's countertop in the bathroom. After a few deep breaths, he turned on the faucet and splashed some water on his face. It was a weak attempt to calm his anger because, until Lenox's face met with his fist, he wouldn't understand this situation any better at all. As he toweled off the droplets, he heard the door to the bathroom open.

She sauntered into the bathroom and turned on the shower. The water pelted the shower wall, and steam rolled from above the glass and nickel-framed door. She started removing her clothing, and it was a sight Takoda found hard to break his eyes away from. He gazed at her reflection in the full-length mirror. And he swallowed hard as she removed each article of clothing from her body deftly and deliberately. With each piece of clothing she pulled off, she began to fold it carefully and placed it all in a small pile on the floor next to the shower stall. His dick strained against his pants, and he tore his eyes away from her reflection to get his mind off of wanting her. He busied himself with placing toothpaste on a spare toothbrush he found in Donovan's linen cabinet.

Her motions became more deliberate than the prior one as she removed her shirt first, followed by her shoes and pants. The last thing to come off were her socks before she was clad in her black bra and matching panties. Toothpaste dribbled from Takoda's mouth as he watched her fluid motions of unhooking her bra from behind her back. Her hips swayed as she shimmied out of her undies.

She caught a glimpse of him gawking at her as she stepped into the warm shower.

"What? It's not like you haven't seen me naked before."

A drip of paste fell onto the counter. Takoda quickly spat out the rest of what was in his mouth and wiped the remaining paste from his lips and chin with a nearby hand towel.

"Well, yeah, I know, but?"

"Shut up and join me—will ya?" she said with a wry smile plastered across her face.

"But?"

"But nothing! I promise I am fine, but I won't be if you become just as complaisant as you were before with making me yours."

His brows knitted as he looked at her through the glass.

"It's only a matter of time before Nayati knows I'm missing. It's better for all of us if you claim me now. Because by law as it is now," her voice trailed as she placed her head under the shower and let out a sigh before shaking her head. "Look, I can't bear the thought of losing you. Take me, Takoda. Claim me as yours because I need you more than anything in this world."

Her face looked like it was about to fall, which made his heart sink to his stomach. No matter what —even if their world was crashing around them, he couldn't disappoint her. Especially since she was right about council law. He peeled his clothing off, and while he placed each article next to her own, her eyes darkened. Once he was fully naked, he got into the shower and brought her close to him. Her pert nipples pressed into his chest, and the sensation alone made his dick harden with desire for her sex wrapped around him. He cupped her ass and plunged his dick against her inner thighs. A moan escaped her lips before he drew his lips to hers.

His kisses started out soft, but they grew needy as she stroked his balls. She moaned into his mouth as she pulled away from his dick momentarily. She then glided her thumb over the sensitive tip.

"God, baby, that feels so good!"

She ripped her lips from his and rained kisses down his neck and stomach before licking his entire length.

"Oh, baby!"

His voice resonated an echo in the bathroom as he tangled his hands in her hair. She felt so good that all he could think about was coming in her mouth, especially once she took all of him in. The mere thought of coming down her throat made his dick twitch with need. Her mouth, teeth, and tongue rubbing, and sucking, and biting all of his sensitive spots all at once made him transcend almost at the edge of pure bliss.

"If you keep that up, I'm gonna come, and I won't do that until I hear you screaming my name."

She released her mouth from his dick, and the absence of her touch instantly made him ache for more of her heat.

"What if I want you to come for me?" She said to him as her fingernails glided over his back.

The sensation sent waves upon waves of electricity throughout his body as his skin became inundated with goosebumps. A low growl vibrated in his chest.

"Bed and now, woman!" He shut the water to the shower and slid the door open. A wave of steam billowed out.

He led her out of the stall and began towel-drying each of her body parts. And all while studying each freckle, birthmark, and scar on her body. Each thought and observation of her beautiful body, he committed to memory.

"You are so beautiful, Treasure. It's a treasure to have you in my life and finally, after all this time." He said to her as he quickly toweled off his own body and led her to the bedroom. Takoda tugged at the covers and gently guided her onto the bed before straddling her.

"You're mine, Treasure, and I want nothing more than to explore every inch of you. But first thing's first." He whispered in her ear before kissing it lightly. "I want the world to know you are mine."

He pressed ardent kisses down her neck until he got to her sensitive spot where her neck met her shoulder, bit down gently into her flesh, and then licked the hurt away with his tongue. It wasn't enough of a bite to hurt, but just enough to leave a mark.

His dick hardened as she let out a moan of pleasure.

"Tell me how you want it, baby."

"Takoda! Please! I need you inside me."

It was all he needed to hear from her. He plunged his cock between her slick folds and began worshiping her sex until she called out his name. She felt so damned good wrapped around his cock that he couldn't deny her a release. And he certainly wanted to watch her come apart beneath him. Still, taking things slower would be fun, too. This way, he could take her further. As he slowed his motion down, she took hold of his ass and thrust his hips towards her.

"Don't you dare! I need, oh—" Her voice broke as her pussy pulsated and clamped tightly around his dick.

The sensation made him want to come right along with her, but he bit back the urge. She was so beautiful while falling over the edge, and he wanted nothing more than to stretch her orgasm out to at least half a dozen more.

"That's it, baby." He said as he stroked her hair and kissed her forehead. "Come for me."

She purred into his mouth as she kissed him, and the sensation vibrated through his body.

"God, baby! You're making me crazy!"

It was music to him and his cougar's ears. He matched Treasure's fast-paced rhythm and found his muscles growing as taut as his dick. Takoda honestly didn't think it was possible for him to get any harder than he already was. Still, she seemed to have found a way to get him there as she wrapped her legs around his waist. He was sucking at the crux of her shoulder now, and as her sex pulsated and grew impossibly wetter, he marked her once more. A faint tinge of copper touched his lips.

"Oh, Takoda!" She wrapped her legs around his waist even tighter than before and dug her mani-cured nails down his back.

He matched her rhythm in response to each of her thrusts as she rode out the after waves of her orgasm. It was only until he panted, spent from pleasing her, that he pulled her on top of him, and she collapsed in his arms.

"You are amazing, Treasure."

He kept his sex inside her as she rained kisses down his neck and chest. The feather touch of her lips made him drift into a relaxing state. He wrapped his arms tighter around her, trying to brand this moment in time with her scent, touch, and the fire in her eyes to his memory.

She smiled at him and kissed his cheek before settling her head on his chest. The sound of her heartbeat lulled him in and out of consciousness for the next several minutes. When he began to almost entirely drift, his cougar took over, and he blinked his eyes open.

Lenox was still a threat, and he could not rest until his Treasure was safe. He looked at her as she lay on top of him in peaceful bliss and caressed her hair.

"No one will ever hurt you again, my love. I promise you that."

"And as your Luna, I promise to make sure no one will ever hurt you."

He smiled at her and was about to pull out of her when she cupped his ass.

"Stay inside me a little longer, please?"

The mere plea had his dick hardening again.

"Baby, if I do that, I'm going to want to make you come again."

"I'm okay with that."

He gave her a cheeky grin before cupping her breasts and rubbing each of her nipples with his thumbs and forefingers.

"Well, in order to achieve that, I'm going to have to make you impossibly wet again. So, so wet."

He thrust his dick into her pussy in unison with each one of her shaky breaths. Her nipples were rock hard, and his dick wasn't far behind. Just looking at the "o" forming on her lips had him thinking about her mouth wrapped around his cock again. Another moan escaped her lips, and this one continued with each rock of his hips. A pool of her pleasure rushed to his dick, which was all he needed. An orgasm began to brew deep within his belly.

"Takoda!"

She kept saying his name as if it was a mantra, and that was something he knew he'd never tire of hearing. She grabbed hold of him and then rolled on top of him.

"It's my turn." She said as she grabbed both of his wrists and placed them over his head. He gave her a pout in protest. "Nope! You don't get to be in control right now. This is all me, and I'm going to ride you until you shout my name loud enough for it to reach the top of Mount Sacagawea!"

She ground her hips fast and hard onto his dick. Each thrust went balls deep, and it was making him so crazy that he couldn't help but match each of her thrusts. Doing so would make him come relatively quickly, and the thought made him a little upset with himself. He'd always wanted to make sure each of the girls he'd been with was satisfied, even when the act was more for him to scratch an itch than anything else. He figured that had more to do with his male ego than anything else. Her thrusts grew slicker, and her pussy tightened around his cock as he continued to match her gyrating hips.

"Mmm... That's it, baby girl! Come for me again!"

Her thrusts and moans and kisses and her continued showering of wetness took him over the edge again. He broke free from her hands and cupped her ass.

"I want you deeper, baby. Cuz I'm coming, and I can't stop myself."

She moaned before responding.

"That's all I needed."

She was pounding against his cock like no other woman he'd had in his bed before. Her pussy clenched again, and this time it was so tight and so dripping wet around his stomach, balls, and thighs that it had him jumping over the edge.

"God, baby! You're so damned wet for me. I love it! I love you!"

"I. Love. You." She said each word with a thrust, and that was enough to have him coming inside her again.

Once they both came down from their orgasms, he pulled her to his side and enveloped her in his arms. The sound of her breathing lulled him into a deep sleep.

SEVEN

A loud knock rang through the bedroom, causing Takoda to shoot up from the bed. He immediately looked over at Treasure, who was still asleep. He stroked her hair and smiled before hearing Donovan's voice through the door.

"Takoda, it looks like they've discovered her missing. They are almost at my perimeter. Get dressed." Said Donovan.

"Be right out."

Treasure stirred in the bed as he tried to get out without waking her. She awoke fully once the warmth of his body left her from under the covers.

"Baby, what's going on? Why are you getting up?"

"They've come." He said to her in a whisper. "Wait here."

Treasure jolted upright in the bed.

"Oh no, I'm not! He's not hurting my mate!"

She rushed towards the bathroom and started shrugging on her clothes.

"Treasure," Takoda started as he pulled on his pants, "I understand you want to stand by me, but things are different now."

"Yes, they are different. You are my mate, and I must protect you."

"You've got a pride to protect now, as well."

"Don't you dare get all technical with me! You haven't announced me as their Luna yet since it just happened. Therefore, by law, I'm not their Luna at the moment—I'm just your mate. And since I am your mate, I will be fighting by your side."

"Yes, I marked you, but you have to admit that's in the loosest sense of the law because you didn't technically mark me because you didn't break my skin. Please, I can't face him if I have to think about your safety."

"This isn't up for a discussion." She said as she headed out the bathroom door. "They outnumber you and Donovan. If I come out with you, we will have the element of surprise and a fighting chance." She opened the door to the bedroom where Donovan was leaning an arm against the threshold.

"Takoda—she's right, and you know it. If you've laid claim to her—even in the loosest sense, Nayati by law will have no choice but to take up his griev- ances with the council. He can't touch her, you, or even me until the council has their say. By then, we should be able to figure out a way to get that staff away from Lenox and destroy it."

Takoda let out a breath.

"Fine, but if there is even a slight indication that Nayati will not honor the law, you need to promise me you will run and head off towards the pride, Treasure. They are in Montana—just outside the border. And Donovan, you must promise me you'll get her there safely."

"Man, stop talking half-cocked! I'm not letting you go up against his entire pride alone, for fuck's sake. No—the plan is that you are going to let us help you! You act more like a lone wolf than an Alpha. Cut that shit out, man!"

"I want to protect you both—how is that bad?"

"And I thought I was bad! I don't need a babysitter! We've all seen war, and we've all survived it. Us against a single pack is nothing!" Donovan said while shaking his head. "Come on. Let's get out there before they are on my doorstep."

THE THREE OF them headed out the front and sat down on the barker lounges on Donovan's front porch. It didn't take long for Lenox, Nayati, and Mika to reach Donovan's porch. All three shifted into human form the instant they saw Donovan,

Takoda, and Treasure. It was a good sign that they'd go by the law, but Donovan gazed at Treasure and Takoda with a knowing look to signify that this meeting could go South at any time.

"I didn't think you'd be so civil with your visit and shift back to human form. We've been expecting you." Donovan said as he crossed his arms.

"We have no beef with you, Donovan. Well, at least right now, since the council has not spoken about who officially leads this territory as of yet. All we want is the girl, and we will be on our way." Said Nayati.

"I'm afraid that is not possible." Said Takoda as he stepped off the porch and walked towards the three of them. Donovan and Treasure followed behind.

"You have no business in this matter. Treasure is the property of Nayati!" Lenox touted while tapping his walking stick three times. It made a large thud when it contacted the earth beneath their feet each time. He directed the staff towards Nayati as Lenox addressed him. "Are you going to let Takoda do this? He is violating the law. We've now got provocation to attack."

"No laws were broken. The girl was promised to me, if you recall, Nayati. Therefore, she is staying with me and as my fated mate."

Lenox's eyes widened.

"You can't claim her. You—you can't claim a

mate who is not of royal Alpha blood! The law is clear!"

"I am well aware of the law, Lenox, and I can assure you that I am within the right to declare her as my Luna!"

"She is part of my pride, Takoda! I did not release her. Therefore—"

"Are you challenging the law of the council, Nayati? You cannot keep a mateless Luna in your pride. You already have a mate, and that is why I am claiming her as mine!" Takoda's words came out as a growl and so low that it even surprised him. He didn't mean to, but his protectiveness over Treasure showed clearly.

"I see no marks on this woman. Therefore I may take her back to wed someone of my choosing."

"First, she is marked, and second, if she were not from royal Alpha blood, you could wed her to one of your Omegas. That is not the case, however. Her father was the Alpha of her pride."

"I want the girl, and I want her now! We must punish her for her crimes against my pride!"

"What crime? Refusing to submit to you? What royal-blooded Alpha or Luna would?" Takoda asked.

"I do not have to explain myself to you! Do not test me." Nayati said as his body showed signs of a half-shift.

"Is that a threat?"

Takoda's voice was now a low growl.

"It is a promise!"

Nayati tried to take a swipe at Takoda with his claws.

"Enough!" Shouted Mika, Nayati's Beta, that remained silent through most of the squabbles these past six months. "The council law states that once a cougar has laid claim to a mate, they have 24 hours to take the matter up with the council—in the meantime, we are not allowed to touch her or them. Am I the only one that understands this law?"

"He has no right, Mika!" Lenox said as he tried to direct his staff towards the man, but Mika stepped further away.

"I have been against your treatment of Treasure and Takoda from the start, my Alpha. Let it be known that I will not be a part of breaking council law." Mika said as he continued to back away from Lenox. He then turned his head towards Takoda, Treasure, and Donovan before continuing. "I promise no harm will come to you by my own hands. I cannot say the same for my Alpha."

"I appreciate that, Mika." Said Takoda.

"My Alpha, Nayati, I don't know what has come over you, but if you do not want me speaking to the council about you breaking the law, I suggest you retreat with me. The same can be said for you too, Lenox. And my guess is that the council will not be as lenient with you as they will be with Nayati. You are a werewolf, after all."

With a guttural growl from them both, they backed away from Takoda and followed Mika back into the woods.

"This isn't over, Takoda! We will take this up with the council at first light!" Said Lenox as he backed away from the three.

Takoda tossed and turned most of the night while waiting for dawn. He then headed out to meet with the council. He wanted to face the council alone, but Treasure and Donovan insisted on coming with him.

"I have a good feeling about this. I think we will get the council to see things our way."

"Well, I'm glad you do, Takoda. But just in case things go south, I want us there as your backup. One against a pride and the council isn't exactly a fair fight—should one ensue."

"I guess you are right, Donovan, but I didn't want to go in there and make them all feel as if they are on the defensive."

"Well, you aren't talking us out of this. We are coming with you whether or not you like it." Said Treasure as she patted Takoda on the shoulder.

The three walked through the forest a bit down the path that led away from Donovan's house and towards the council's place northeast of Nayati's compound on the other side of the mountains.

The trio was about to enter the council's quarters when Nayati and Lenox greeted them.

"Honestly, I didn't think you'd show," Lenox said as he opened the door to the quarters and motioned for them to enter. "Figured that you'd bail."

"You know that isn't our style, Lenox."

"You couldn't face becoming a shifter when Ocean first claimed you. That's why you ran here to Wyoming in the first place, Donovan. I don't think you have any room for talk."

"Enough! We, the council, will decide the fate of these prides! And we will do it in your silence, Lenox!" Spat the highest member of the council, Motavato. "You will only speak when spoken to. Do we make ourselves clear?" His eyes grew as dark as his inky black pin-straight hair.

"Yes, your Grace." Said Treasure as she bowed before them.

"Ms. Treasure, I'm glad you understand the severity of this situation. It is a huge and serious accusation that has been cast on you and the shifter that is stealing you from your pride. What have you to say about this?"

"Your Graces, it is true. Takoda is my fated mate."

"But Takoda is not a member of your pride. Also,

he cannot mate with just anyone. His fated mate must come from royal lineage. You do understand the laws—don't you?" Said Motavato with knitted brows.

"Yes, and if your Graces allow me the chance, I can prove to you all that I am Takoda's rightful mate."

"Very well, you may speak."

"During the Civil Were War, my entire pride was killed, including my father, the Alpha of our Cheyenne pride just south of the mountains. My father was Jacy Black."

Motavato gasped.

"He was your father?"

"Yes, your Grace, Motavato."

"And you kept it from us all. Why?"

"Because upon seeing me during the war, it was law to kill the Alpha and any family members who could rightfully become an Alpha."

"Yes, that was the law during the war, but it is different now. Why did you wait for so long to tell anyone?"

"I blocked the horrible memories out of my head. It wasn't until recently that I regained such memories. And since Nayati promised me to Takoda's pride once I was a full-fledged adult, I thought of Nayati's pride as a foster one. It wasn't until Nayati forbade me from seeing Takoda that I realized The Bourgeoning had occurred. I could renounce him as my Alpha—something only a true Luna of royal blood can do."

Motavato's eyes widened.

"Is this true, Nayati?"

"Well, yes, I mean," Nayati's voice trailed slightly as he stepped away from Lenox to address the council.

As he did, Lenox took a few steps closer to Nayati and placed his staff within Nayati's view. He lightly tapped the staff on the wooden floor, and the sound made a chant-like vibration that echoed the four walls of the chamber.

Donovan, seeing this, stepped around everyone until he was behind an unknowing Lenox.

"Nayati, the law is very clear about this. Once you discover a shifter you've taken into the fold from the war is of Alpha blood, they must mate. You don't have an available Alpha to mate within your entire Cheyenne pride."

"Yes, I understand," Nayati started again. His voice shook along with his head. "forgive me, your Graces. My head is a little—I'm not sure?"

Nayati palmed his knees.

"I feel like I'm going to faint."

Another light tap from Lenox's staff shot through the room. Donovan reached from behind Lenox and grabbed the staff out of his hand.

"Just what do you think you are doing, Lenox? You know it is illegal to be practicing the dark arts in council chambers." Donovan said as he moved the staff out of Lenox's reach.

"What do you mean? This is an outrage, your Graces! I demand that you make Donovan give me back my staff at once! I'm an old man, and I need it for walking!"

Before the council could protest, Donovan broke the staff in half, and a visible dark green mist was dispelled from the staff. Nayati blinked several times before shaking his head.

"What is going on? Why am I here at the council chambers?" Nayati asks as he rubs the back of his neck. "And why does my head feel like it is about to explode?"

"Do you not remember bringing up charges against me?" Asked Treasure.

Nayati shook his head again and screwed his eyes shut before responding.

"The last thing I remember clearly is the day we were planning your initiation into Takoda's fold." Nayati's eyes widened. "And that was the first day you showed up!" Nayati said as he pressed his index finger into Lenox's chest.

Motavato's expression hardened.

"Lenox, what do you have to say for yourself?" Motavato said as he raised a hand to Lenox before continuing. "And choose your words carefully! Because we all saw that dark green mist dispelling from your staff. So it is clear you have broken more than one law of this council today alone. No one—not even an elder may perform magic on Alphas without the council's permission! That is the difference between us cougars and you werewolves. We are civilized! If you hadn't performed that blood oath, the Civil Were War might never have started."

A low growl formed within Motavato's throat as he spat each word. "You will take the word of a lone wolf and an Alpha of a Shoshone pride over mine? I'm the true leader of the Cheyenne ancestors of this land. You appointed me, after all."

"Clearly, your intent is malicious. I know what magic is, especially when I see a spell breaking before my own eyes. Do you have anything relevant to say before this council passes down a judgment on your actions today? And those of the past six months by deceiving our good intentions to take you in as a refugee." Spat Motavato.

Lenox reached inside his robe and pulled out a vial. Donovan tried to grab it from Lenox, but Lenox threw it to the ground before Donovan had the chance to retrieve it. A large gray cloud appeared and enveloped Lenox. Once the cloud dissipated, Lenox vanished from the council chambers.

"Damn it," Nayati said. "Where did he go?"

"I'm not sure, but we are going to find out. We must stop Lenox before he causes more trouble to the packs and prides. Wars follow wherever he is, and the shifter community can't have that any longer. Your Grace, Motavato, will you send word to Lenox's son Gavin and his mate Fallon about what has happened here." Asked Donovan.

"Yes."

"Good." Donovan nodded and let out a long breath.

"Motavato, your Grace," Nayati said as he bowed his head before continuing, "I am deeply sorry for my actions, and I will take full punishment for my crimes."

"Nayati, you were under the influence of a dangerous spell. I cannot hold you accountable for what Lenox did to you. Please, just go in peace and prepare for this Luna's Bourgeoning because I expect to be invited to the Mate Bonding. Once it is official, of course." Motavato said with a smile. "Thank you, your Grace. We will prepare at once."

The four left the council chambers and were about to head back to their compounds before Nayati stopped them.

"Takoda, Donovan, I owe you both an apology. Treasure, I can't tell you how sorry I am for everything I've done. Bits and pieces are returning to me now that the fog is lifted from my head. I can't believe I hurt you." Nayati said with glossy eyes.

"Nayati, none of this is your fault. That's why I've been so adamant about not wanting to fight you. Both Treasure and I knew Lenox was up to something. We just didn't know what until we pieced everything together a couple of days ago. We weren't completely certain until Lenox started banging that stick around." Nayati's eyes widened.

"Where is that staff now?"

"The council has it, Nayati—well, what's left of it, anyway. I'm sure they will dispose of it properly. Everything will be fine. You'll see."

"I hope you are right, Donovan. But I still can't help but worry." Nayati said. "Let's all head home. We have a Mate Bonding to prepare for."

Treasure started to follow Nayati off to the left as Donovan and Takoda went towards the right of the path.

"Treasure, when I said, let's all go home—I meant you as well. You should be with Takoda today so you can prepare for your first hunt with him tonight." Nayati said with a smile as he patted Treasure on the shoulder.

Treasure smiled back and headed over to Takoda, who enveloped her in his arms.

"Nayati, thank you." Said Takoda.

"No, it is I who should thank you all. If it weren't for the three of you, I'd still be under Lenox's spell. And once he'd gotten what he wanted with all of you, he'd kill me and take over my pride. We'd probably be facing another war."

Nayati nodded in their direction, waved, and turned on his heel to head towards his compound.

Donovan, Treasure, and Takoda watched him walk until he disappeared into the thickness of the forest.

"It's over, right?" Treasure asked as she let out a breath the instant Nayati disappeared into the woods.

Takoda pulled her into his chest and gave her a squeeze as he kissed the top of her head.

"Let's hope but knowing Lenox? It isn't."

EIGHT

oth Takoda and Treasure said their goodbyes to Donovan as soon as Sonya greeted him with open arms fifty feet from his property line. They then walked down the short path to Takoda's Shoshone pride compound. He wasn't surprised by all the cheering as they entered because he had already told Viho that all was safe for the pride to come home. What did surprise him was to hear cheers for him to present their Luna to the pride.

"Viho, what is all of this?"

"You didn't expect me to withhold the fact that someone is finally going to make an honest man out of you—did you?" Viho let out a chuckle as he clasped his Alpha on the shoulders with both palms.

"I guess not."

Takoda turned to Treasure and palmed her

shoulders, guiding her towards the center of the pride, now forming a circle around them.

"My pride, allow me to introduce you to your Luna, Treasure."

The crowd roared in response.

"Hi, everyone." Treasure said while waving a hand in front of the crowd.

Once she put her hand down, the crowd dispersed towards the main area of the compound. Some started a sacred fire, and others set up tables and chairs for the hunting ceremony celebration.

"Takoda, why don't the two of you get some rest before the ceremony tonight? I'm sure the two of you have had little sleep in the past few days."

"Yes, that sounds like an excellent idea. We will meet all of you back out here around nine in the evening."

Takoda took Treasure's hand and led her to his place in the compound. As he opened the door, Treasure's mouth was agape.

The living room was decorated in tasteful leather and wood decor. It looked put-together rather than sparse like she typically saw in a bachelor's space. Each piece of furniture and artwork looked sophisticated and strategically placed. Almost as if he had help from a designer.

"I don't know about you, but I could use a drink. White or red?"

Treasure smiled as her eyes darted all around the room. There was so much to take in.

"Wine? Ah? White would be good." She said as she caressed the buttery, soft, dark brown sofa. "You have a beautiful place."

"Thanks. Though I must admit, I watch far too many of those home shows—that's why my living room doesn't look like a college dormitory. The kitchen isn't as nice as this, though. Kitchen's next month's project."

"So, are you like a designer?"

Takoda shrugs his shoulders.

"Contractor. It keeps me busy, but yeah, sometimes I flip houses. I've got an entire pride to feed. Hunting in a state forest is generally frowned upon." He said with a wink.

"Well, you are fantastic at this. Lots of subtle pops of color and lots of texture."

"Thanks. Come on, the wine's in the fridge in the kitchen."

Treasure followed him into the kitchen as he pulled two wine goblets from his cupboards.

"You were right about the kitchen." Treasure said as her eyes darted to the stovetop and wall oven that screamed the decade of 1960 in all of its avocado-colored glory. The wine fridge seemed to be the only thing in the space from this millennium. "I take it this place hasn't been renovated in this century yet?"

Takoda laughed as he opened the bottle of wine and poured a heavy-handed helping for them both.

"Yeah, we came here about six months after Donovan settled in. It was a good place to stay away from humans since the population had dwindled to one. Not that we need to avoid them because all of my pride are born shifters, but it's just so much easier to keep to ourselves to avoid exposure. An older couple owned this ranch previously, along with all the land surrounding the place. So, once they passed away and it was on the market, I bought it to make it into a compound for the tribe. Been living here ever since. But I will say that the others' quarters are more up-to-date than mine."

"You are really talented! I wouldn't know the first thing about building a house."

"It's rather easy once you understand what you are doing. But enough about that! Let's have a toast to us!" Takoda said as he brought his glass towards Treasure's.

The pinging sound between the glasses filled the kitchen. Treasure smiled and brought the glass to her lips.

"This is really excellent wine." She said after downing the entire drink in one gulp. "I know I should sip it, but after the past couple of days, I'm sure you can't blame me." She snatched the bottle and poured herself another glass.

"No, I can't blame you for that, but I hope you

aren't that quick with the rest of the night's festivities."

Treasure raised one of her brows.

"What are you talking about? I thought we had a ceremony with the pride tonight."

"We do. But I meant before that," Takoda's voice trailed as he inched closer and slipped an arm around Treasure's waist. "I planned on some alone time with you." He pulled her waist to his.

She felt the hardness of his erection pressing against her inner thigh, sending shivers throughout her body. Goosebumps littered her skin as he traced a line from her cheek down her neck with his index finger. His finger stopped when it reached the top of her cleavage, peeking out of her button-down shirt.

"I want to kiss every inch of this gorgeous body of yours, Treasure. I'm starting with here." His words were a faint whisper before his lips grazed just above the tops of her breasts.

He unbuttoned her shirt, pulled it off her shoulders, and pressed light kisses down her neck and exposed shoulders.

"Then I'm going to move to here." Takoda continued as he slid the cup of her bra off her breast and kissed the exposed skin. "And I'm going to pay extra attention to this." His lips hovered over the tip of her breast as his warm breaths teased her nipple to attention.

She moaned softly as she pulled him closer to

her chest. Her fingers then fumbled at the button and zipper of his jeans. He shimmied his hips to help her quickly pull them down his thighs, exposing his fully erected dick. She took the gigantic mass into her palm and stroked it as he continued to suck on the taunt nipple of her breast.

"I'm going to get the tub going." He said after a few brief moments. "You relax here with your glass, and I'll bring the bottle into the master suite for us."

She let out a sigh the minute he pulled away from her.

"I'm gonna follow you. I don't think I can stay away from you for that long." She said with a wry grin and a wink.

"Okay. Follow me if you wish." He said as he grabbed the bottle, and they went down a long hallway from the kitchen leading to the opposite side of the home.

He opened the door to his master en suite, which was also handsomely decorated with muted off-white and royally hued gray tones. Her gaze became fixed on the French doors leading out into an area flanked by a covered hot tub. Her eyes widened as he opened the doors leading out to the tub. A garden oriental in nature surrounded the tub with beautiful green and red hues, sporting the ornamental grass and leaves of the Japanese maple.

Treasure's mouth grew slightly agape as he pressed a button on the tub to remove the cover.

"When you said you would get the tub ready, I didn't think you were talking about a hot tub."

Takoda shrugged.

"I figured since I don't enjoy being around humans all that much that I'd make my backyard into the oasis I always envisioned in my head. Plus? I like the bubbles." He said with a wink.

"Oh, I'm sure. It's just I figured we'd be in the bathroom." Her face flushed. "This is outside where we are naked," she swallowed hard, "and exposed."

He put his arms around her.

"Treasure, no one can see us, but if you'd rather, we can go back inside—"

"No—no! I'm fine with being here with you. I didn't know if the pride bothers you while you are out here or anything."

Takoda laughed.

"They know better than to bother me, especially today."

He cupped her cheek and claimed her lips. The kiss was deep, urgent, and seemed to brand her very soul with his. She had always known that he was her mate, but it wasn't until now that was she sure her love and passion for this man were as in sync as her cougar was with wanting him as hers and hers alone.

He slid her shirt off and all the while keeping his eyes locked on hers. His lips kissed her collarbone, hitting the one sweet spot that always made her knees buckle and her body shiver with pleasure. He pulled his lips away, and instantly Treasure felt a chill from the absence of his heat. When she finally opened her eyes, both he and she were completely naked.

He scooped her into his arms and lowered her into the hot tub. Warm bubbles surrounded her legs as she glided her body onto the seat by the right edge of the tub and reached for her wineglass to take a sip. The jets massaged her sore back and eased her tension into a relaxation she had never known until now. He sat next to her with a glass in his hand.

"I propose another toast to us." He said as he tipped his glass towards her. The clinking sound resonated within the backyard as the bubbler continued to make calming, gurgling sounds.

They both took a sip and placed their glasses on the tub's edge. Takoda cupped Treasure's cheek and kissed her forehead.

"You are so beautiful, my Treasure. I want you, baby, and more than anything in this world right now."

His voice lowered to a guttural growl as he pulled her into his arms and trailed kisses down her neck to her chest. Palming one of her breasts in his mouth, he sucked on the nipple to make it peek at his attention.

She let out a soft, almost inaudible moan and

then bit her lower lip as she put some distance between the two of them to gain her composure.

"Babe, you can be as loud as you want here. Everyone else in the pride is at their own place, which isn't within earshot of here." He said with a chuckle while running his fingers through her hair. The sensation made her relax into the touching gesture. He kissed her cheek before whispering over her ear. "I like it when you scream my name."

His other hand glided down the length of her body, and it rested in her lap briefly before he plunged a couple of fingers into her feminine folds. She pulled his body over hers and ran her fingernails down his back. A low growl stirred in his chest. He arched with pleasure before he thrust his cock deep within her core, and he continued to worship her sex until they both came undone and spent from pleasure.

NINE

She woke to a loud bang coming from directly outside Takoda's bedroom. They'd hunted for only half of the evening and turned in earlier than the rest of the pride. The past couple of days had taken a toll on them, and they wanted to get some sleep.

Still blurry from sleep, she squinted her eyes to get her vision to correct itself and focus them in the noise's direction.

The backyard was secluded from the others, Takoda had assured me. So why does it sound like someone is back there?

When they made love in the hot tub earlier, she couldn't see any weakened entry point—something she'd grown accustomed to looking for during the war.

The sound came again. This time a voice followed the loud banging.

"Takoda, I will not rest until you face me, you coward! Come and fight me for this land and territory!"

The voice was all too familiar to Treasure. It was Lenox, and he had apparently come to fight Takoda. Treasure placed her palm on Takoda's chest. She was going to shake him awake gently. But before she could, Takoda shot up out of bed.

"Stay here." He said to her as his lips brushed her forehead before peeling the covers from his body.

He didn't bother putting on clothing. Instead, he immediately shifted into his cougar form.

Treasure had seen him in this form many times before, but his coat seemed to glisten more in the early moonlight this time. His eyes, usually a greenish-yellow hue, seemed to take on a bit of a blue tone that matched the color of the moon's craters at night. She didn't know Takoda when he was a kitten, but given this hue, she assumed his eyes were this gorgeous even back then.

Takoda, I can't let you fight him alone. As your mate, I want to stand by you.

Her cougar was the one who was talking at this point—even though she agreed. Treasure wouldn't ever back down from a fight, and she had an innate need to protect her Alpha mate.

A twinge rose deep within her belly, and it was a

sensation she hadn't ever before experienced. She clutched her stomach as if she was instinctually protecting it from harm. Takoda palmed the hand that held her stomach with his paw. He then began kneading her palm and then tummy covered by her PJs in gentle strokes.

No! Please stay here and protect yourself, our pride, and the child that grows within you. I know you felt my seed take root—I did too. Please, Treasure! Stay here. It's the only way that I can face him. Because I will then know that you are safe.

"I'm here, my Alpha." Said Viho as he knocked on the bedroom door.

Guard our Luna with your life. She's now bearing the future Alpha of this pride!

Treasure could hear the words, but they sounded as if they were coming from a muffled microphone. Everything was utterly surreal to her at this point in time. She felt the shot of energy surge through her as Takoda released his semen within her when they made love in the hot tub. Still, she wasn't completely positive that she was pregnant, and it would take at least two weeks for a test to conclude all of this was true.

A shiver rushed her spine. She didn't want her Takoda facing Lenox—regardless of her circumstances.

Takoda! No! Can't we just run?

He nudged her cheek with his head while purring.

We can't this time, nüttüühai ~ nittüühai. He would kill anyone who tried to escape the compound, including Nayati and his tribe. I must face him. I have no choice.

"What is your decision, Takoda? Almost sounds like you are going to be a coward!"

Takoda leaped out the door. His long legs landed within two feet of an unshifted Lenox.

"You know the laws! Why do you come at me fully shifted?"

You are the one that challenged me, Lenox! And on my land! I have every right to face you in my cougar form! That is the law too!

Takoda was hissing and growling as he slinked closer to where Lenox stood.

"Only cowards face an opponent in shifter form!"

Are you going to talk your way out of this fight, or are you actually going to fight?

Takoda knew Lenox was stalling, but he wasn't sure why.

"Fine! I will shift just as soon as we make the ground rules! If I win, your Luna, your pride, and your land are mine!"

Is that all?

"What else would there be? This land is prime real estate to own the territories in the middle of America! Why wouldn't I want it? And as far as your

Luna goes, she has power, and I enjoy aligning with power. She'd make powerful babies too."

Let's discuss if I win, then.

"Fine!"

If I win, you become rogue and banish yourself into exile. You are never to bother with any established packs or prides. This is the law stated in the war treaty, and you will have to abide by it!

"You can't be serious! That law hasn't been enforced."

It hasn't because shifters like you are now fewer and farther between. Contrary to what you believe, shifters really do want to get along with one another. Oh! And so we are clear, this is a fair fight! You and me only—no one from our prides can intervene. So, do we have a deal or not?

Lenox shifted before answering the last question —which to Takoda only meant one thing, Lenox wouldn't be playing fair. His black fur bristled as he growled and snapped in Takoda's general direction. All of Lenox's actions still made it appear as if he was stalling. Takoda lunged into the air, baring his sharp teeth, aimed straight at Lenox's throat.

Before he could connect with Lenox, Paco and Sahale, members of Lenox's pack from the north, came at Takoda from both sides. Their teeth pierced Takoda's flesh. He tried to shake them off but wound up in a tumbling scuffle with them both. The two kept scratching and biting him in all directions, and Takoda found it difficult to keep a focus on Lenox.

As the two pulled him on his back, he saw Lenox enter his bedroom. Now in human form, Lenox wrapped his palms around Treasure's throat.

"If you won't be mine, then I'm going to make damned sure that he can't have you either!" Lenox spat. "Say goodbye to your Treasure, Takoda!"

"Treasure! No!" Takoda squirmed to escape both werewolves. Still, they held on tighter and forced him to watch Lenox as he slowly squeezed the life from Takoda's entire world.

Nayati's large cougar suddenly leaped over the fence and into Takoda's backyard. He knocked both dogs off of Takoda. Lenox's eyes widened at the blitz attack and released his grip slightly around Treasure's neck. She, still in human form, kicked Lenox in the groin. Lenox stumbled backward and cupped his family jewels, freeing Treasure completely from the chokehold he had on her.

Treasure and Viho shifted into their cougars and joined Takoda and Nayati. All barring their teeth in the intruders' direction. Behind them was a growing number of Nayati and Takoda's prides climbing and jumping the fence leading to Takoda's backyard. Knowing they outnumbered him, Lenox took to his shifter form, jumped over the wall, and ran off with his tail between his legs. Sahale and Paco followed Lenox as all three disappeared into the night.

Cheers roared through the crowd as each tribal pride member shifted back into human form.

Takoda ignored the cheers and rushed to Treasure's side.

"Are you hurt? I should hunt him down and kill him for touching you!"

"Takoda, I am fine." She said as she cupped his cheek. "There's no need to chase after him. Let him go. He knows he's defeated."

Takoda pulled her into his arms and held her tight.

"Let's head back into the house so I can tend to your wounds." Treasure said to Takoda.

"Considering what happened tonight, perhaps we should have the handfasting in a couple of days and forego the two-day hunting ceremony." Said Viho to Takoda.

"That might be best." Said Takoda as he guided Treasure back towards the house.

Viho opened the gate to the fence leading out of Takoda's backyard so the others could disperse throughout the compound to prepare for the handfasting.

She glanced at the mirror again to make sure everything was real. It had felt that sometimes this day would never come, but here she was in the bathroom getting ready to marry Takoda in front of the entire pride. She took a deep breath to squelch the tears of joy welling in the corner of her eyes before she opened the door to head out to the compound's front courtyard.

Gardenias and fairy lights lined a makeshift metal arbor that Takoda was standing under with Zhang, a sorcerer, and friend from the Northeast that they called over to perform the handfasting.

She walked, as they had practiced, slowly towards the arbor. Treasure was never great with heels, and since she was now pregnant, she felt even more awkward with them. Those things would be flung somewhere the first chance she got after the ceremony.

She finally reached a smiling Takoda.

"You look beautiful." He mouthed to her while moving closer to her and taking her hands in his.

Zhang smiled before starting.

"Dearest friends and family, both Takoda and Treasure have brought us together on a joyous day. Today, we've come here to show these two beautiful people our love and support! To celebrate them as they join their lives together in marriage and mating. Marriage and the mate bond aren't something to be entered into lightly. Uniting two paths into a single journey requires us to be thoughtful, intentional, and honest. Marriage brings with it a deep realization of our responsibility and commitment to our partner, and the understanding that love, loyalty, compassion, and compromise are the foundations of a happy and enduring home." Zhang looks toward Takoda before continuing. "Takoda, do you come here today to marry Treasure and join your path with hers?"

"I do."

"Treasure, do you come here today to marry Takoda and join your path with his?"

"I do."

"Takoda and Treasure will now exchange rings and the words they've written for each other. These words are promises they make to each other, to keep each day of their lives together."

"Treasure, I knew you were special the first day I met you. You were someone I wanted to protect and teach the ways of the pride. At first glance, I knew then that I needed you in my life and in any form that you'd have me. And now? Now that we have grown in love together, I can't think of being without you for any longer than taking a breath. You have made me the happiest man in the world today by becoming my mate, my Luna. I promise to cherish and respect you always. I promise to care for you and protect you. I promise to comfort you and encourage you. I promise to be with you for all of eternity." Takoda said as he placed the platinum band on Treasure's ring finger.

"Takoda, I too knew from the start that I needed you in my life. I am so lucky to declare that you are mine in front of our pride family. Ever since the first day you came across me in that cave, your love and trust have made me a stronger and better person. And that love and trust grow and deepen each day I get to spend with you. You were there for my greatest challenges and all of my greatest achievements. You encouraged me to grow as not only a person but also as your Luna of this pride. You helped me believe in myself and become the person I am today. I know I can do anything in your arms and by your side. I'm proud to call you my husband

and my Alpha." Treasure said as she placed the platinum textured band around Takoda's ring finger.

"And now, both Takoda and Treasure have asked us to join them in a handfasting to symbolize that their union takes place on a spiritual and physical level."

Zhang takes the ribbon from the gold plate and wraps the cord around their clasped hands.

"Handfasting is an old tradition. With each wrap of the cord, you deepen your commitment to each other, vowing to respect and support one another. And grow with each other, offer each other compassion and understanding, and take each new challenge and adventure as it comes, together. Let this bond be strong and loving! By the authority vested in me by the Shifters Council, and the State of Wyoming, I now pronounce you the Alpha and Luna of your pride! Takoda, you may kiss your bride."

Takoda claims her lips. Cheers and hollers surrounded them. They break from the kiss and walk down the makeshift aisle, hands still held together with the rope. Once they reach the aisle's end, Takoda turns to the pack.

"What are we waiting for? Let's get this party started, shall we?"

Takoda picks up a glass from a table set up with wine flutes and raises it to the crowd as the pack is handed glasses of their own.

"To a new beginning!" Takoda said.

As the glass touches his lips, an all too familiar wolf leaps in front of Takoda and strikes him down.

Since she is now married to you, I guess she will die by your side. I don't take leftovers.

Treasure dropped her glass of cider in shock that she could still hear Lenox, and Lenox shot her a look.

What's the matter? You thought the telepathic bond between us would break when you decided to leave? I'm afraid it doesn't work like that with a practicing were-witch! Now fight me, Takoda!

Takoda remained in his human form.

"Bite me."

That can be arranged.

"You can't be serious, Lenox. We completely outnumber you, and not even the council will not back you up on this. They are here if you want to take up this business with them now. An act like this will probably land you in a holding cell or worse. We could have Zhang neuter you and ensure it sticks for good this time. You've lost, rogue. Face the facts that Wyoming is not your home."

Lenox leaped into the air and outstretched his paw to swipe at Takoda. Takoda stepped to his left, and Lenox's body hit a nearby tree.

"I don't wish to kill you, Lenox. Go back to wherever it is you crawled from under and leave our prides alone."

Lenox got up from the ground, shaking his head, and turned back into human form.

"You will regret not fighting me now, Takoda."

"Is that a threat?" Takoda said with a chuckle.

"It's a challenge! Killing you later will bring me great joy."

"You know better than to cause trouble, Lenox!" Said Zhang as he finally reached the group.

"Zhang, I should have known you'd put in your two cents. I don't have to answer to you—none of you!"

"You have no power here, rogue. Leave Wyoming, or we will force you out!" Said Donovan.

"You will all regret this day. Mark my words." Lenox reached into his robe and pulled out a vial before continuing, "Even my son will fear my wrath!" He said as he smashed the vial at his feet. Smoked billowed from the vial and consumed Lenox. Once the smoke cleared, Lenox was gone.

Takoda faced Zhang and Donovan.

"Is this something we should take up with the council?"

Zhang patted Takoda on the shoulder.

"Not today. Lenox isn't strong enough to be a threat. His pack is far too small to take us all on. Besides, we have a union to celebrate!"

Takoda smiled and pulled Treasure into his arms.

"You are right, my friend. You are right."

Music began to play, and Takoda and Treasure found themselves surrounded by the pride. Takoda took Treasure in his arms and swayed his hips to the music playing.

"I love you." Treasure said as she placed her head on Takoda's shoulder.

"And I love you. You will be my Treasure for always and forever."

THE END FOR NOW

BEFORE YOU GO...

Enjoyed the book? You can sign up for my newsletter where I offer more fun!

I promise I won't bombard you with tons of emails! I generally write them once a week or once a quarter depending on my writing schedule!

https://www.authoramandakimberley.com/newsletter-signup

IF YOU LIKE LOVING THE ROGUE YOU MIGHT LIKE...

THE *Pride* WITHIN

USA TODAY BEST SELLING AUTHOR

AMANDA KIMBERLEY

THE PRIDE WITHIN
CHAPTER ONE

"Damn it!" Levi shouted for what seemed like the hundredth time in the past few minutes. "All I'm asking, Google, is for a search that comes up with my uncle in it. Is it really that hard for you?"

He pounded his fingers against the keys in protest to his Ancestry search. All the while he wondered if the hard taps would break the keys. That wouldn't be a good thing since his keyboard was attached to his computer laptop.

"God! This is pointless!" He screamed as he closed the computer. "And what is it going to accomplish anyway? It's not like my parents ever talked about Uncle John. They never talked about any of the family!"

He picked up the letter his cousin sent him and pulled out the obit. As he traced the photo of his uncle with his index finger, he hoped to get a tangible connection. It was hard to believe his own image stared back at him from the paper. An uncle that looked THAT much like him should have been more prominent in his life. But being his parents broke off ties to the family, it became impossible for him to connect with his great uncle. Anyone with Reis blood seemed a perfect stranger now that he'd become an adult.

The problem wasn't so much his parents as he got older, and he knew that. The blame fell on himself once he got into his twenties. He didn't try to find a way to reach out, and that fell squarely on his shoulders. His grandparents would have been the best bet for getting reconnected. They always hosted early family Sunday brunches that lingered throughout the day. And those visits would have gone into the evenings if his extended family didn't have to take a 2-4 hour drive back home.

None of them lived too far away from Levi while growing up. His grandparents and parents lived in a rural part of Connecticut. Not too far from any major cities like New York, Boston, New Jersey, and Philadelphia. The places where all his relatives lived. He always had legitimate reasons for not visiting his grandparents. And he felt guilty that he didn't have the time to come visit them and the rest of the relatives as he got older.

Life seemed to get in the way when it came to studying for college exams. And working 2-4 jobs to go to college made things difficult. His friends vying for what was left of his time made things worse. In college, the friends won out and he'd find himself hanging out with them until the sun came up on most weekends.

A thought of his best bud Judd Nelson hit his mind, and a smile washed his face. The dude always needed a wingman for the ladies. Levi obliged the request since he got his pick when hanging out with Nelson at the local dives.

Judd's skills at scoping out the ladies when they'd hang out to shoot some pool and darts proved legendary. Levi liked the women Judd picked. These consistently cute women never looked for any long-term attachments. This suited Levi fine because he didn't wish to look for anything permanent either.

He brushed over the obit picture again and read the paragraph they had on his uncle. He seemed to be a loner like Levi because the paragraph made no mention of a wife or kids. Levi frowned a little as he wondered if he'd wind up sharing the same fate as his uncle. At the age of 27, he still had no desire to tie the knot.

Who am I kidding?

He opened up his laptop again and logged into his Facebook account. He went into the photo tab and scrolled until he found Tara Winston's picture.

A half-smile formed on his face as he remembered the two glorious weeks they dated two years ago.

She wasn't any prettier than the other girls he had dated, but special in her own right. She was like the girl next door, a girl you'd take to meet your mother, and he wished he didn't let her go. But at the time he was only interested in thinking with the head between his legs. And he knew that that girl deserved more so he broke it off quick.

Even though he would have loved to see how things went, he had no plan of marrying her. He had no intention of marrying any of the girls he dated. He only wanted to have some fun and not be so lonely.

His apartment was about as empty as a bachelor's place would be. There weren't any paintings or pictures on the walls. No tchotchkes on his coffee table. No plants or even a pet. He only had functionally comfortable furniture in his living area and a flat screen. He didn't need anything else.

The kitchen was just as sparse. He wasn't much of a cook unless heating frozen dinners were some kind of culinary art. He only owned a set of four flat dishes, drinking glasses. And none of them matched. Matching stuff was something a girl does for dinner parties. Dinner parties weren't his thing. Judd was the only one who'd come over. They drank from beer bottles, so fancy frosted mugs weren't a priority.

Levi shut the laptop once more and headed for

his bedroom. He kicked off his dress shoes and flicked them into the open closet. A large space that only contained two other pairs of footwear, a pair of sneakers and a pair of cowboy boots. He then slid off his tee shirt and jeans and shoved them in a crumpled pile next to his shoes and hopped into his bed. It was just as plain as the rest of his place. He only had it on a simple bed frame with no headboard. His bedding was all black from the sheets to the comforter. The only other piece of furniture in the room was another flat screen.

He flicked on the TV and scrolled through the channels until he settled on the movie John Wick. When Keanu Reeves discovered his dog had died, Levi was already asleep.

ACKNOWLEDGMENTS

Most readers believe that writing a story is mostly a solitary thing. I mean, sure, you have your characters that keep you company, hold you hostage if they don't like the scene you are writing about them, or sulk if they really aren't a true villain in your story and want a happy ending for themselves in a sequel.

Truth be told, all of these things have happened to me over the four decades I've been writing. But? Other great things have happened too. Fabulous friendships with other writers have developed over all of these years, and I am grateful for every single one of them.

Thank you, Sarah, for always having my back and always, always believing that I can write. You are a wonderful publisher, author, and friend who challenges me to always do my best.

Thank you, Michy and Mel, for always being my cheerleaders. Even the *Other Side* can't keep the two of you from helping me reach my goals. You've filled me with your vast experience in this business when we were all content writers who were just trying to make a few bucks for our babies, including the fur and feathered kind.

To my Connecticut author friends, Dale and Jamie, who have now become family. Thank you for continuously checking in with me, and you are always willing to *talk shop*. You've both been a soft soundboard for me to cultivate my ideas before I really run with them.

To Christie, girl, you've been on this journey with me since the content writing days, too. But not only are you a fantastic author that inspires me and pushes me. You've also been an unbelievable friend while we've been riding this rollercoaster called authoring. Sometimes it isn't the characters or the story that gets us stuck, it's life getting in the way, and you've taught me not to feel guilty when I need to take a step back for a perspective.

Finally, to Cheryl, the first fan who emailed that wasn't blood-related to me. You've been a beacon that I strive for. You've been a reason I get up in the morning and rush to the computer to write. You've been a friend. You've been a fellow *fibro fighter*. I don't think I can ever thank you enough for being there since *way* back when. And *still*! You are around today as my loyal, faithful cheerleader and calming voice that gets me through some of my muddled thoughts.

About the Author

USA Today Best Selling and award-winning author Amanda Kimberley has written in various genres in the course of almost four decades.

Her nonfiction blog, which focuses on the chronic disease fibromyalgia, has garnered recognition from various organizations, including Health Magazine. Naming her blog, Fibro and Fabulous, as a top blog for fibro sufferers.

Amanda has also written for medical magazines and sites like FM Aware, The National Fibromyalgia Association's magazine, and ProHealth.

When Kimberley is not writing nonfiction, she enjoys penning romance. Her first Furry United Coalition story, The Turtle and the Hare, earned the 2020 Summer Splash Book Awards of Ink and Scratches for Best Romance. Her Forever Series Books, Forever Friends, and Forever Bound were featured in 2015 and 2016 on the BookCountry website, a division of Penguin/Random House as editor's picks. She has also been featured as a USA Today Happy Ever After Hot List Indie Author with

Claiming My Valentine, a Best Poet of the 90's ranking for an anthology, and has had a #1 PNR ranking with Immortal Hunger and Hearts Unleashed.

Amanda Kimberley is a Connecticut native that now lives in the warmth of Northern Texas with her zoo consisting of her husky, tuxedo cat, mice, rabbits, guinea pigs, a tank of fish, two daughters, and a husband.

When she is not writing you can find her cooking whole foods for her pack. She also enjoys reading, hiking, and gaming.

facebook.com/authoramandakimberley

twitter.com/KimberleyLB

instagram.com/amandakimberleylb

bookbub.com/profile/amanda-kimberley

ALSO BY AMANDA KIMBERLEY

PNR Series

The Forever Series

Forever Friends

Forever Tied

Forever Cherished

Forever Bound

Forever Immortal

Forever Blood

(Coming Soon)

Forever Loved

(Coming Soon)

Forever Yours

(Coming Soon)

Forever Mine

(Coming Soon)

Historical PNR Series

The Witch Journals Series

Salem's Trial by Judge

Salem's Trial by Township

Salem's Trial by Birth

(Coming Soon)

The Gypsy Witch Trials

(Coming Soon)

Colonial Witch Trials

(Coming Soon)

Stand Alone PNR

The Cure

Manifestations

Uncharted

The Pride Within

Co-Author Stand-Alone PNR

By the Pool with Alex Kimberley

Scifi Fantasy PNR

Suburban Shifter & Celestials Series

Loving the Alpha

Loving the Lone Wolf

Loving the Loup-garou

Loving the Rogue

Loving the Lykos

(Coming Soon)

The Equipoise Solar System Series

Laying Claim to the Lion

(Coming Soon)

Laying Claim to the Legacy

(Coming Soon)

Laying Claim to the Original

(Coming Soon)

The Pandemic Series

Pandemic Passion

Pandemic Pandemonium

(Coming Soon)

The Season of Shifters Series

Midnight & Mistletoe

Midnight & Magic

(Coming Soon)

Midnight & Memories

(Coming Soon)

Midnight & Mergers

(Coming Soon)

RomCom PNR

The Eve L. Worlds Hellenic Island Shifter Series

The Turtle and the Hare

The Turtle and the Rock

The Ferret and the Fossa

The Leopard and the Llama

(Coming Soon)

Contemporary Romance

The Chronic Collection

Down by the Willow Tree

To Hell With Carpets

Welcome Home

The Chronic Collection

The Just Series

Just Breathe

Just Believe

(Coming Soon)

Just Be

(Coming Soon)

Nonfiction Self Help

The Fibro and Fabulous Series

Fibro and Fabulous: The Book

Fibromyalgia and Sex Can Be a Pain in the Neck

Fibromyalgia and Pregnancy

Poetry

Blue Water Baptism

The Puzzle Called Life

For More Information Please Visit: https://www.bookbub.com/profile/amanda-kimberley

* 9 7 9 8 8 3 7 9 3 1 8 4 0 *